A little bit Dirty

WILLOW WINTERS

From *USA Today* and *Wall Street Journal* best-selling romance author Willow Winters, comes a second-chance story with a filthy-mouthed, possessive hero, not willing to lose the love of his life again.

I've got a thing for men who work with their hands.

I thought I'd learned my lesson by now. But here I am, back in the small town I grew up in, staring down the man who broke my heart years ago.

I intended to tell him off.

My plan was to flip him the bird and prove to both of us that he hadn't ruined me.

I sure as hell wasn't going to sleep with him.

Until he tells me he's sorry.

Until he gives me that smoldering look I still dream about.

Until he whispers just beneath the shell of my ear... His breath trails down my neck and he leaves an openmouthed kiss right there, in that sensitive spot.

"You have no idea how much I've missed you."

My treacherous heart wants more. More of him. More of us. But there's a reason it didn't work before and when you don't learn from your past mistakes, you're bound to repeat them.

A little bit
Dirty

Prologue

Asher

Five years ago

"I THINK YOU'RE STUCK NOW," ROBERT comments with a smirk. *The pull tab of the aluminum can snaps and the sound is finished off with the familiar fizz that's a constant on the top floor of the hangar. He takes a sip of his drink and then looks back at Brianna. Motioning toward her with the cheap beer can, he laughs and says, "She's got you tied down, and the whole town knows it."*

The smile that grows on my face is easy. My girlfriend has this quirk of knowing the moment I look at her. Doesn't matter if we're at school, in her backyard or in the hangar, she just knows. The second my eyes land on her, she turns around as my gaze moves from her flowing skirt, trailing up her body to her face. She stares back at me with those gorgeous green eyes of hers, a soft simper playing on her lips.

Readjusting in my seat I give her a short tip of my chin which makes her blush, and she turns back to the group of girls.

She's sweet, shy and petite and no one would know it, but she's damned determined. She gets what she wants and right now, she wants me. Bri peeks at me while the group laughs and there's this look in her eyes that's been there for a few months now. It's a look that makes everything else fade into the background, and I swear it silences everything to the point where I can only hear my heartbeat.

A second passes and then another that slows the whole damn world down. I could get lost in her, and I think it's the same for Bri.

"For Pete's sake, get a room," Renee chides and it takes me a moment to realize Robert had gotten up to give Magnolia a kiss. She's all sorts of red and even though I notice her through all the laughter on the top floor of the hangar, I can't keep my eyes off Bri. I play along, hollering out and joking, "We've got a room in the back!"

Bri never stops looking at me, and I can't stop looking at her either. She might not like the attention, but one day I'm going to kiss her in front of everyone in this small town too. There's no doubt in my mind. I love her, and she's going to be my wife.

Present time

I wish I could go back to that moment. Where we were only naive kids but at least knew what love was. If I could go back and get down on one knee right then and there, I would. 'Cause she would have said yes. She would have been mine and then when my world collapsed, she wouldn't have let me push her away.

If only I'd known I was going to lose her, I'd go back and I would promise her my forever. She loved me then … I still love her now.

"Hey, you hear me?" Robert's voice comes through the receiver of the phone and I clear my throat before telling him, "Yeah, I heard."

Brianna came back to our small town.

"I just wanted to give you the heads-up," he tells me as if anything at all could prepare me for this.

Chapter 1

Brianna

FATE HATES ME. IT WANTS TO EMBARRASS ME, humiliate me, shame me, hurt me.

That's the only conclusion I can come to as I slam the car door shut in frustration. Even that is done weaker than I'd like on this far too hot morning. It only closes with a dull thud and no one seems to notice that my world is crumbling.

Turning over the ignition a dozen times didn't even give me a tick, a purr, not a thing. The keys jangle in protest as I throw them into my purse and stomp up the cobblestone street back to the bakery's awning so I can at least be in the shade. My heels nearly slip and I struggle to keep my composure.

All I can think is now I have to see him. My heart races quicker with every passing second.

Practically falling onto the wooden bench perched on the stone walkway in between the bakery and the florist, I take in a steadying breath and attempt to find any solution that keeps me far away from Asher.

Instinctively, I dial my sister's phone number again and it rings rings rings; all the while I glance down the street. Her children are young; I love them to death but they are a handful, so I'm not surprised if she's busy wrangling them up. Or maybe she's already at work. It's nearly eight fifteen now. The shops have opened their windows, and the streets are only occupied by a few cars ... the town is coming to life.

And inside I am dying.

There isn't another mechanic around for at least two hours. My car is dead in front of Melissa's Sweets and I'm stuck here, in a long-sleeved dress that's already damp under the armpits. It's autumn and beautiful in South Carolina, but not cool enough for my favorite burgundy cashmere drop waist dress. It's my good luck dress ... or at least it's supposed to be.

Dropping my head back, I let out a frustrated groan. I could sit inside the bakery and commiserate there, but right now, I just want to be alone.

It's my first day of work. Luckily, it's in my mother's realty office, so I'm not too concerned. More embarrassed than anything. I'm sure everyone knows my parents gave me the job simply because I'm their daughter. They wanted me to come home and a job is the stability I needed after going into debt studying business at college. I knew I could get ahead if I took the handout. Yet here I am, first day, and running late.

Freaking great.

The call to my sister is met with her voicemail. Just as my mother's phone was.

I'm quick to check my texts and Renee's last message reads: *Just call him.*

"Him," as in, Asher.

Renee's a good friend, and honestly I'm surprised she's even awake. She's a bartender and the last of my contacts I texted … simply because I thought she'd be sound asleep.

I text back in a flurry: *Isn't there anyone else?*

Her answer is immediate: *It's a small town. You know that.*

The response strikes me like a blow to the heart and I know exactly why. It's me, not her.

For the longest time after we broke up, that's what I told myself. That we were only together because Beaufort's a small town. Because options were limited. I lied to myself and I knew from the very moment that thought registered it was nothing but a lie. He was my first but so much more than that. He was the one who made me smile and laugh when things were hard, or even when they seemed impossible. Asher was my partner in it all. He was the one I wanted to hold hands with until the day I died. My best friend. He was my everything.

And then one day, I was nothing to him.

I almost text Renee that I'm more than aware it's a small town and that's why I almost didn't come home. *Almost.* But the same reason I wanted to stay away is exactly why I'm back here in Beaufort. It's small and filled with gossip, and everyone knows everyone else's business. At the same time, all of my family is here, along with all my friends who I've known since before I can remember.

… and the first and only man I've ever loved. The one who broke my heart. My fingers play with the small charm at the end of my necklace. My nervous habit has always been to fidget with it and I'm quick to lower my hand. Inwardly I'm still fiddling with the pendant I always wear.

Tears prick at the back of my eyes and I'm quick to shut that down. I knew it would be hard coming home. I knew it would hurt even. I just don't want to deal with it. Definitely not alone.

I hesitate to ask, but I can't help myself so I text Renee: *Could you come pick me up?*

If I'm going to have to call him for help, I at least want Renee here. She's the strongest of us all. No nonsense and she also knows everything. There were rumors when we split. Plenty of people said lots of things … but Renee knows everything. She knows every sordid detail and she still loves me.

I send another text, hoping she can tell how desperate I am: *Please?*

Chapter 2

Asher

"**Y**OU'RE FUCKING WITH ME, RIGHT?" I joke on the end of the phone, casual and lighthearted. Huffing a laugh like it's comical. It's not, though. All this phone call has done is shred me up.

"Nah man, she called us. I told her we were two hours away and she said that was fine." Nathan drones on the other end about how his team can't waste the gas and tells me he's referring her to me.

Everything in my chest is tight as I tell him not to worry. That I've got this.

But damn does it hurt. She's been back in town for weeks now. My gloves come off one at a time after hanging up the phone. They fall to the counter with a thud and I turn around, leaning my back against it and steadying my thoughts. The scents of oil and rust fill my lungs with each deep breath. Everywhere I look in this place, I see her.

Hell, our first kiss was right there to my side, against the now faded red tool cabinet.

She may have left but her memory never did. With the ghosts of our past lingering in the garage, I grab my keys as fast as I can and get the hell out of here.

I'll get this over with. That's all I keep thinking, but that doesn't explain why it feels like the beginning and not the end.

I'm halfway there when I realize the radio is off. The rumble of the engine and the faint echoes of my memories were all I had for a good fifteen minutes. The moment I flick the volume up, though, dead set on shutting down the jumbled thoughts, my phone rings.

I don't know why I thought it would be her. I'm out of my mind to think it, but I do. With a long exhale I answer the phone. "Hey man, what are you up to?"

Robert answers, more upbeat than usual which is my first sign that things are off, "What are you doing tonight?"

"Nothing that I know of except working." Aptly, *work work work, all day long,* plays dimly on the radio as I keep driving.

"Something's going on at the Iron Brewery

downtown … Bri's going to be there." Robert's last state-ment is spoken carefully. Like he's not sure what that information would do to me. Encourage me to go, or keep me far away. I decide to put him out of his misery.

"I'm actually getting ready to see her now," I tell him and realize I'm only a couple blocks away now. It's been years since I've talked to her. Years. How the hell did that happen?

"Really?" The surprise is evident and unfortunately hopeful.

"Not that she's wanting to see me …" Clearing my throat I add, "Her car broke down."

"You do it?" Robert says, his slight Southern drawl emphasized by the joke and then he adds, "You empty out her gas tank or something?" His quip gets a genu-ine smile from me and the huff of a laugh.

It's the only relief I've felt since the phone call this morning.

And it's gone in an instant.

Sitting at the stop sign, I glance to my left and there they are. Renee's taller and Bri's standing right beside her, talking with her hands waving as she always does.

Renee's in her pajamas still it looks like. She couldn't care less what this town has to say about decorum and I've always liked that about her. She's a passing thought, though. All I can focus on is Bri. It's only the ticking of the blinker and Robert's question that brings me back. "You still there?" he asks.

"I've got to go."

"Call me if you need me," he says and I hesitate, not knowing what to say. I don't need him. There isn't a thing he can do for me.

I need *her*.

My throat goes tight as I turn left into the central strip down Main Street. I've done this a thousand times in my life, but this feeling—this prickling, numbing sensation—is something entirely new. It's like dread and hope mixed in a drink, all washed down with regret.

I can barely look at Brianna, yet I can't take my eyes off of her just the same.

Everything about her is familiar.

I know I've unzipped that dress from her before. Kissed the crook of her neck as the cashmere fell down her shoulder. Fuck, my cock is already hard remembering her. Remembering us and the things we've done together. The things I've done to her.

As I park parallel to the sidewalk with her car behind me, I peek into the rearview mirror and her green eyes find mine. There's a spark and a jolt, but they're quickly followed by a hollowness as she rips her eyes away, turning her body toward Renee and crossing her arms.

I don't miss the concern on her face, or the eagerness that radiates from her to leave. Hell, if we were only kids, I bet she'd take off. She'd leave her no-longer-dependable sedan and haul ass around the corner so she wouldn't have to see me.

I give myself a moment, leaving the truck idling before climbing out and letting the door slam shut.

My footsteps are heavy, like they're trying to keep me from moving to her at all.

"Hey," she answers so hesitantly, I barely hear her.

"So, it won't start," Renee states with a wave of her arm. With sleep still in her eyes and her strawberry blond hair in a messy ponytail, I'm pretty sure she would rather be in bed.

"You just roll out of bed for this?" I ask her comically. Wanting to ease the tension. I don't feel a hint of it from Renee, but Bri's acting as though she'd hide behind her friend if she could.

Renee doesn't answer other than a laugh.

"So it won't start?" I ask Bri and she peers back at me.

The cords of her neck tighten as she swallows and the world slows down. There's silence between us as she struggles to answer such a simple question. We're feet apart; me in the parking space, her on the sidewalk. My hands in my pockets and her arms crossed over her chest. The last time we were this close, though, I broke her heart, so I understand why she's guarding it now.

I'm sorry, is right there on the tip of my tongue.

"Yeah, it just died," Renee answers and my gaze moves to her, my brow raising. I can only nod as I look back at her, avoiding Bri's stare.

My thumb runs along my stubbled jaw as I glance down at the asphalt, then back up to Bri and tell her, "Look, if you want to—"

"It's just the car, Asher. Please, just … if I could have called someone else, I would have. I'm sorry."

Her words are hushed as she readjusts her stance a dozen times, her insecurities rolling off of her. I don't miss her fidgeting with her necklace. Old habits die hard.

I knew I hurt her. Fuck, it hurt me too. But seeing her standing there, hating being near me when for my entire life all I wanted was to be close to her, fucking kills me.

"I'm sorry," she repeats and then pushes her hair behind her ear, letting her arms fall to her sides instead of crossing them over her chest again. "It's just, the car won't start. I didn't want to bother you with it … I know we don't talk or … I just … it's a small—"

This time I'm the one to cut her off.

"I'm aware you moved on, Bri. I'm only here for the

car," I tell her as easy as I can, not letting an ounce of emotion in. As if there's nothing to be emotional about. As if she doesn't have to feel guarded around me. I even manage a smile that feels fake as hell.

Swallowing thickly, I open up the door and grab the keys from where she left them on the passenger seat. I'm more than aware that the two of them are staring at me. I'm sure Bri's head is filled with a million thoughts right now. A million things she'd like to say to me.

More than half riddled with profanity, I'm sure.

But all I can think as I prepare the car to tow it away is that somewhere deep down, maybe she does miss me. Maybe there's a piece of her that feels the way I do.

That thought is the only thing that keeps me moving after I look up and see both of them gone.

Chapter 3

Brianna

I F I'M CONSTANTLY WORKING, THEN I DON'T HAVE to deal with all of these thoughts that badger me. During the week I'm the new secretary for my parents' realty office on the outskirts of town and on the weekends, I'll work here. At Tammy's Salon. Aptly named after the woman who opened it two generations ago. Although her granddaughter Sarah now runs the business.

That's the way it works here. My grandfather opened the realty office and now I'm working there. The lakeside fishery has always been run by the Johansens and their family. John's great-grandfather started the funeral home … I suppose someone's got to do it. Everything passes down from generation to generation.

"I think, just a trim," Kimberly says, pursing her

lips as she stares at her brunette hair in the floor-length mirror in front of us. She's a kindergarten teacher who only ever cuts her hair whenever there's a wedding, but she comes in regularly for a style. Her father was a high school teacher and he retired just last year. Her mother still runs the floral shop. When people say everyone knows everyone in a small town, they aren't exaggerating.

"Right around two inches?" I ask, her thick hair between my pointer and middle finger as I hold it up for her to see. It's like déjà vu. Kimberly was one of the first clients I ever had, although the chairs were different back then.

With a bright smile she nods and says, "That'll do it."

This part-time gig was easy to fall into. I worked on the weekends when I was in high school too. It's almost as if I've never left.

With one obvious exception.

Asher. With a quiet yet deep inhale, I give the nylon cape a couple of flaps and then wrap it around her chest, snapping it shut in the back.

"So, how are you settling in? Is it nice to be back home, or do you miss the big city?"

Big city. I don't miss feeling alone while surrounded

by so many people. I keep that thought held back as I bite the inside of my cheek to keep from speaking.

"It's good to be back," I tell her with a smile and lead her back to the sink to wash and condition her hair.

The sound of the running water competes with the hum of chatter in the salon. A genuine warmth floods through me. It really is good to be back. I missed my family. My sister especially and my mom too. They came up to visit often while I was in college, and my sister would call me almost every other night just to chat. Still, it's different.

There's something about the place you call home that's comforting. It's the things that are familiar maybe, but really it's the people.

This salon is the perfect example. It's changed. The main room is the same size it's always been, with the sinks in the same place, but the entire space has been given a fresh paint job. Creamy purple covers all the walls except the one with the stations and mirrors, which is a complementary shade of darker purple. Sarah said it's called Soulmate. She also outfitted the booths with antique white carved wood drawers and copper finishings. It's both high end and quaint at the same time.

The decor is nothing like the old salon that was here when I was in high school. In that way it's different, but they're just superficial changes. It hasn't changed a bit when it comes to what really matters. Mrs. Harding still demands her hair be permed in rollers. And gossip still fills the salon. It's still a place for low-key therapy sessions too. Although I should be the one seated in the chair if that's what I'm after.

Given the dead weight in the pit of my stomach, that's exactly what I need right now.

"You good?" Amber questions before chewing her gum in the corner of her mouth. She's busy drying her client's hair with a towel but her eyes don't leave mine.

"Fine," I answer a little too high pitched. She gives me a half smile and a knowing nod that I am anything but fine.

That's what I tell everyone. I'm fine. Fine is a good place to start, isn't it?

"So Magnolia's got a new man, I'm sure your sister filled you in," Kimberly tells me as I massage shampoo into her scalp.

"Oh, I heard." I heard all right. It's all Autumn could talk about for weeks. When I was just a kid hanging out with my older sister, Mags would often be there too. They liked hanging out with me and Asher because his place always had beer. His parents didn't mind if we were drinking, so long as we stayed the night. So I got to be friends with people in the classes ahead of me and that included Magnolia Williamson. When her father passed after embezzling money from investors, it was all anyone could talk about for the better part of a year. I have to admit, hearing she got her happily ever after feels like this town got its just desserts. "The scandal of the century," I murmur with a touch of humor.

"Good for her, I say," Kimberly says and smiles. "I think they make a beautiful family."

I nod along, feeling that familiar warmth again although it doesn't last long. I just can't get over what Asher said and I need to talk it out. I swear every two minutes I think about it.

Voices drone in and out and Kimberly complains about something that happened during the last school board meeting. I swear they should televise those things with the drama that ensues.

All I keep thinking about is how Asher said he knows I've "moved on." What exactly does that mean? 'Cause I'll be honest, there isn't a piece of me that feels like I've moved on. He might not love me or want me; he might not think it's a big deal anymore. But it is to me.

My phone vibrates just as I've finished blow-drying Kimberly's hair and I'm quick to check it. It makes no sense that I thought it was Asher. My father told me he dropped off my car at the house already. Asher had my car for two days and didn't message me once. He spoke to my father instead. I know it's 'cause Renee asked him to, because I asked her to relay that request. I don't know why I thought it would be him texting me now.

It's only Renee messaging me back. Earlier I texted her: *What does he know? For him to say he knows I moved on, what exactly does that mean?*

Renee's reply is short and it makes me feel like I'm obsessing. Like I should let it go: *Why does it matter, Bri?*

With my heart sinking even further than it already was, I concede. She's right. It shouldn't matter.

I text her just that at 3:08: *You're right, it doesn't matter.* Setting the phone down, I ignore it and every other thought about him for the rest of the day. I settle on the "fake it till you make it" approach. It doesn't matter. The past is in the past for a reason.

It's only when Sarah's locking up with Amber, who keeps asking me if I'm okay, that I read Renee's replies which came one after the other.

3:10: *That's not what I said, Bri. It's okay if it matters. I was asking, why does it matter to you if he thinks you've moved on? It's a good question to ask. Why does it matter to you what he thinks or thinks he knows?*

3:25: *Hey, I love you. I think my message came out wrong. Text me back, please.*

4:50: *If you don't text me, I'm dragging you out to the bar tonight.*

5:25: *All right, well I hope you like what you're dressed in, 'cause you're coming to the bar with me later. No buts. I'm picking you up before work and getting you drunk tonight.*

Chapter 4

Asher

THE BAR STAYS OPEN THE LATEST. WHEN ALL the shops are closed down, the streetlights shining, and the workday is over, the bar is where everyone comes to take a load off. To have a drink and a laugh, and not worry about a damn thing.

With a Red Bull in my hand, I take a look around and I know every soul in this place. That's what I like most about it. At the old bar, the only one that used to be in town, I liked the booths with the cracked seats. I liked the wood floor and I liked the bar with its pitted top. This new place Brody and Griffin opened is more like an upscale pub. Expensive counters, and everything is new and shiny. If I'm honest, I like this place just as much as Charlie's Bar and Grill. 'Cause the voices that fill it are all the same.

I like hearing my friends talk to one another. It's comforting, having people around. Faces you know. Jokes you hear once or twice. My ma said I've always been a people watcher, and I've always loved to help. So it just makes sense to come to the bar where we can simply be.

They're all working on taking the edge off or are on their way to tipsy. A few of my friends will drink a bit too much, but there's always someone to drive them home.

It never used to get to me, but after my dad got sober, I just haven't been able to trust a drink myself since then.

Nobody knows what happened with my dad. He's a backwoods kind of guy and bars were never his thing. Sometimes I wonder: If he had drunk at Charlie's with friends and people close to him who could have seen it coming, would it have gotten as bad as it did?

Taking a sip of my energy drink everyone thinks has vodka in it, I push that thought away. It's no use wondering. The only thing that matters is that the truth stays hush hush.

My mother doesn't want the world to know. So I smile, I carry on, and my family secrets stay just that: secrets.

"You need another?" Renee asks. I nod but ask for

a Coke instead. Renee's usually quick to fill drink orders, but she lingers a second longer, eyeing me with a
sly look on her face.

"You say hi to her yet?" Renee asks and then glances
down the bar before filling a glass with soda.

A heat races down the back of my neck as I take the
drink from her. The bar is only so big and the moment I
walked in here, I felt her. Brianna is like my North Star.

"Was just about to." Somehow my voice is even as
I answer her.

Renee can't hide her smirk and I wait a moment,
thinking she has some advice or a joke, knowing her,
but she only nods and goes about her business. It's busy
enough in here that she doesn't have time for small talk.
Still, I wait a beat longer before pinning my focus on
Bri.

The girl I loved has become a woman who wants
nothing to do with me. And I know it's my own damn
fault.

She belongs here, in this town and in this bar. She's
what makes the whole place complete. Like what it's
supposed to be. I don't know how to explain it other
than she's who I want to be here more than anyone else.
I've always been comfortable here in my hometown, but
there's nothing like when she smiles. That's when it feels
like this is where I'm supposed to be. The last two years

have been hard, too fucking hard, but I didn't realize just how heavy it's been till she came home.

In a pair of light blue skinny jeans that are ripped at the knee and a simple black silk tank top, Bri leans over the bar and orders herself another drink. Her ass is right fucking there, wrapped in denim and begging for attention. Clearing my throat, I wrap my hand around my glass of Coke, watching her shamelessly. I can't seem to stop myself. How can I, when I haven't looked at her this way in two years?

Is she thinking of me right now?

The other bartender, Denver, pushes her drink across the bar top, and Bri pulls it in close. Her slender fingers wrap around the glass and then her lips wrap around the straw.

When her lips curl up, I know damn well that she knows what she's doing. Little vixen. Maybe the alcohol warmed her up, or maybe she's gotten over the anger she felt when first seeing me—I don't know what it is, but I'm happy that she's bothering to notice me at all.

Then she turns and looks me in the eyes. "Stare much?" she asks, with a little smile that seems designed to drive me crazy.

We haven't been together in years. Now that she's back home from college for good, it's legal for her to drink like this in public instead of back at the hangar.

We're allowed to be here in the bar together. Only we're very much not together. I can't decide whether to be relieved she's where I can see her, or nervous to talk to her. Bri's buzzed. She's having a good time. She's still looking at me, waiting for me to speak.

"Come here." I tap the spot next to me at the bar. The chatter in the rest of the place washes over us.

Bri raises her eyebrows. "Why?"

"I want to talk to you."

"Is that so?" Her hand curls around her drink. She takes a sip, then a longer one. It's not her first drink of the night. Looks good on her, though. Heat in her cheeks. Eyes bright.

"It is so. Come here so I don't have to shout."

"You're not shouting now," she argues.

It's not very loud. It's mostly our friends, and they just want to have a nice time. Twenty, maybe thirty people in here. It's loud enough that she could scoot closer, though. Especially given what I want to tell her. The topic of conversation isn't a fucking car, I'll tell you that.

"Come here," I say again.

Bri looks at me for a long time, then slides down the bar and steps closer. It feels like a heavy weight in my chest has lifted simply from how perfect she is. On my next breath, I catch her sweet, floral scent in the air. She smells just the same. It's been years since we've been together like this and I think she uses a different shampoo now, but overall, just how I remember. There's something about her that I would know anywhere. I breathe it in without being obvious. Memories come flooding back, along with those feelings, all of what we used to be.

It's almost how it used to be. We were so damn close. To each other. To a life together. A surge of regret forms a lump in my throat and I swallow it down. What was I ever thinking, pushing her away like I did? Hell, I knew the moment I did it, I shouldn't have let her go.

Her wide green eyes peer up at me and the playfulness is dimmed. Maybe without space and an audience she's regretting acknowledging me at all. "What do you want?" Bri asks softly.

"I wanted to have a conversation."

"About what?" She's less brash now that she's closer. A little shyer. She takes another sip of her drink, her eyes not leaving mine. "After all this time, you decided you had something to say?"

"I always have a lot to talk about with you." I slip my hands in my pockets, hoping she knows how true it is. Hell, we lost what we had because I kept everything in. If I could go back … I'd let it all out.

Bri's drunk, biting at her lip, and I can't stop myself.

"But mostly I wanted to hear your voice. Even if it's for you to tell me to go away."

She chuckles soft and low, this feminine sound and a smile lights up her face at my joke. She peers up at me and I can see it like a dare, like she's going to tell me to go away in a way it's obvious she's just playing around, but she bites her tongue.

Proof that we're both holding back.

"You could tell me something else, though," I'm quick to say and shrug.

"You just want to hear my voice? You want me to tell you a story?"

"Yeah. About you. Tell me about work. What it's like being home."

A beat passes and then another. The emotions swing left and right. For a second there's a flash of awkwardness between us. Old, unresolved pain. Bri takes a deep breath. "I'm going to be working at the salon on the weekends and with my parents at their place during the week."

"Two jobs … college must've cost a pretty penny," I joke.

She makes a dismissive sound and twirls her straw in her drink, the ice clinking as she does. "You could say that. But also I want to save up. Get off on the right foot, you know?"

I nod and keep my thoughts to myself. I poured every penny I had into the garage. I made a backwoods mechanic shop into a thriving business that meets the town's needs for a jack-of-all-trades handyman. The debt I understand, though.

"That's right. Save up and then spend it all. If I remember right, that's how you do it."

"It's true," she says with a little laugh, catching herself getting all passionate about the subject. Her voice is a soothing balm. Especially her laugh. It's better than anything I can imagine. I still feel the same way when I hear it.

"It's good to have you home," I tell Bri.

"It's good to be home," she admits and there's a shift between us. It's gentler, like her guard has dropped more than a little.

She relaxes more on the stool and I take a side step, getting a touch closer. I could rest my arm behind her, leaning against the low back of her seat, but I decide not to.

"What about you?" she questions. "Is the shop everything you dreamed it would be?"

There's a pang of nostalgia that hits me when I nod. "It is."

"You're good at fixing things," she comments and

there's a softness to her tone that's hard to place. Then she goes back to sucking down the last of her drink.

"Yeah, I like it. It's nice when something's fixed in the world."

Bri makes a little sound like I hurt her as she sets her now empty glass down. "Is that what you're doing tonight? Fixing something?"

Us, I want to say. She already knows it. She served that question up fast and easy. I broke what Bri and I had between us, and it's the one thing I can't fix with all my tools. It's the one thing I don't know how to fix. All I can think to do is get her close to me. That's how I start, anyway. I put my hand around her waist like I wanted to and pull her in.

Half of me's scared out of my mind that she's going to resist me. She could shove my hand away and pretend we never met. But Bri doesn't. Her body molds to mine without an ounce of resistance. She studies my gaze. My whole body's hot.

"Feels less broken now," I murmur.

"Does it? I don't know." Brianna swallows hard. "You know, it is a little loud in here." Her voice is barely a whisper. Tension crackles between us and this I recognize. The heat we share, and the way her fingers lay on my thigh.

Bri baby. I remember those little touches and exactly what she wants me to do when she gives them to me.

"If you want, I'll take you somewhere quiet." Somehow I keep my voice even, although adrenaline and desire mix together like a drug in my veins.

Every nerve ending is lit and I'm all too aware of every small move she makes.

"Yeah," she agrees. "Could you take me somewhere so we can talk?"

Bri lets me help her off the stool, to the back of the bar, and down a narrow hall. For months I helped get this place in order, so I know every inch of this building. Griffin might have something to say if he saw me back here, but he owes me one. More than one, actually. So I keep us going, determined to leave the bar closer to Bri than I was when I got here.

I steer us into a storage closet filled with cases of beer, barrels, cups—all sorts of shit stacked up against the walls. Shoving the door shut and locking it, I turn to face her.

"I locked it," I tell her and she takes a step forward, then a hesitant step back. Like she's unsure. "No one's going to interrupt."

The only thing I'm sure about is us.

You want to hit me, yell at me? Go for it, Bri. You want

something else, go for that too. The words are right there on the tip of my tongue, but they go unspoken. I'm too damn scared to say the wrong thing.

"What were you doing out there?" she says in a breathy voice, eyes flashing. Like maybe she wants to fuck me, or maybe she wants to hit me. Hell, maybe she wants to do both at the same time and I wouldn't blame her. "What the hell are you doing, Asher?"

"What are you doing?" I fire back, but my voice is low and tempts her.

A flush hits her cheeks as she inhales. "I was just out with my friends. I'm having a good time. And you're kind of ruining it," she says. Her tone is anything but confrontational, yet her statement throws me off.

"I'm ruining it? How? By talking to you?"

"No. You're ruining it because you're sitting at the end of the bar looking all hot." Her emerald eyes pin me in place when she adds, "And I want to kiss you. All I want to do is kiss you."

"Kiss me, then," I challenge, knowing she's not going to and hoping she will anyway.

Brianna is on me in an instant, pressing her body against mine in the narrow space. She kisses me without holding back. Her lips mold to mine and urge me to part my lips with a suckle and a nip. She tastes like sweetness and alcohol, her body tight against mine.

In a quick move, I push her into the wall between a pair of heavy-duty storage racks, and she writhes against me like the drink finally set her free. Like she's been holding back for far too long.

I'm harder than I've ever been. She's all too aware, her hand gliding down my length as she leans her head back and I'm able to kiss her neck.

She moans my name and then her hand is at the back of my head, demanding I kiss her again. Her fingers rake through my hair and I fucking love it. I love everything she does to me.

We crash into each other, and I almost knock over a case of beer while we shove clothes out of the way. Bri spreads her thighs and I push inside of her with one hard thrust. She's already primed for me, wet and eager. If her pussy is anything to go by, my Bri was in desperate need. It happens so fast, I hardly register I'm fucking her until my jeans are in a pile around my ankles. I'm immediately lost in her. I need more of her before I can take another breath. She's so damn sweet and soft and her mouth is on mine and it's all I've wanted for two years.

With her back against the wall, I brace her where I want her, wrapping her thighs around my hips and angling her just right to fuck her hard and deep.

The small strangled moans fuel me to fuck her

harder. If I was thinking straight I'd wonder if anyone could hear us, but I'm not. All I need right now is to feel her come on my dick.

Little gasps pour out of her mouth with every thrust. She's hot and feels fucking perfect. It's the sweetest sex I can imagine up against the back wall of a bar.

Music filters through the door. Our friends laugh. Brianna moans against my shoulder. She throws herself against me and I lose the last part of me that had any doubts.

I try to hold back and slow down. I try to make this last. It's not like we can stay in this back room forever, but damn, she feels too fucking good. The moment I realize I'm close, my thumb works her clit.

"Come for me, baby," I growl in the crook of her neck.

I'll be damned if I come without her. It's just that she's wrapped around me tight like her body never wanted to let go. And yet—she's so ready for me. Like she's been hot for this since she walked into the bar. I refuse to even breathe until she hits her climax.

"God, Bri," I groan, "you feel so fucking good."

Her murmured response is incoherent as her heels press into my ass and she comes hard and fast.

The moment I feel her orgasm, I want another and another. Her nails dig into my skin and she bites my shoulder. I keep fucking her, riding through her pleasure and praying she'll get off again.

She cries out my name, a little too loud, and I leave openmouthed kisses down her neck.

Bri kisses me back along the side of my neck, and her warm breath tickles down my shoulder.

I push deep inside of her, taking every inch for myself. Bri switches to moans instead of words. I can feel how close she is to coming again. Closer and closer and closer.

"Give it to me, baby," I command her as I spread her legs wider to fuck her deeper, harder, and faster. I coax her into it. Kiss her passionately until she shivers out pleasure all over my length. Brianna comes with her face buried in my shoulder, crying out, and God help me, at the same time I lose myself inside her, I can't help but think, *I hope they all heard her screaming my name.*

Chapter 5

Brianna

WHAT WAS I THINKING?

Really, what made me go into that back room with him? I'm the one who said it. I'm the one who threw myself at Asher.

What the hell was I thinking?

I know him. If I said I wanted space, which I do, he would have given it to me. If I said I just want to get settled and figure things out, he would have said he understood. If I said I didn't want to be alone with him because I don't trust myself, he would have made sure there was someone there the entire time.

'Cause that's the kind of man Asher is. And apparently I'm the kind of girl who leads him on …

It's all I can think, all day and into the evening. It's

a beautiful night, and I'm out on my back porch with my sister and my friends. It's the best kind of evening.

Technically it's Sunday, but we're hanging out like it's Wine Down Wednesday. The girls, drinks and gossip. It's supposed to be laughing and having a good time. All of them are chatting away. My sister and her crowd of friends, Mags and Sharon. And Renee of course.

Mags isn't drinking and her little bump is looking a little bigger now. The glow of pregnancy suits her.

They laugh and that's when I get the hint that I should be laughing too.

All I can think about is Asher and how I might have just made a very difficult situation even more difficult.

I followed him right into that back room and then pounced on him. Every detail is vivid and I knew exactly what I was doing.

If another second had passed without me kissing him, I think I would have died right then and there in that bar. How was I supposed to wait with the way he was looking at me, like no one else existed? With his hand on my waist? Forget it. We weren't going to have that conversation in front of everybody.

Turned out to be not much of a conversation. Just sex.

With the ice clinking in my sangria, I readjust on the wicker patio chair and revel in the sweet lingering pain between my thighs. Amazingly hot sex. Like the kind you see on TV.

My cheeks heat at the same time my phone pings. He's been texting me, and I haven't answered. Just as I start to feel bad about it, another text comes in. His name, lighting up my phone screen. I bite at my lip, trying to figure out what to say to the man who broke my heart.

Another text comes in from Asher.

Asher: *I want to talk. Just answer me, baby.*

When I was with Asher, I was weak. Any little thing he wanted, I did. And hearing him call me baby again, seeing it written here ... it makes me soft.

He might miss me, and I might miss him, but I am terrified that I'm going to be naive when it comes to him again and he's going to break my heart a second time. I'll hand it right back to him if he asks, and then it's his to throw away if he wants.

I type out *I miss you too*, then delete it. All day it's been that. The right words simply aren't there.

What are we getting ourselves into?

I can't be a mess again. I won't go back to that place. And there's an easy solution to prevent it: don't let this man back in.

I can't trust him not to do it again. And ... I want to

talk to him, because we were best friends for so long. It would probably be easier to trust him. But I can't. That's how I got hurt. I trusted the wrong person.

"What's going on with you, Bri? You've barely said a word since you got here." My sister nudges me with her elbow. I peek up from my phone and they're all looking at me. My whole body goes hot. With the expressions on their faces, I'm almost certain they know exactly what I'm thinking.

"Yeah," Renee agrees. She leans against the porch railing, her brow scrunched in question. "You do seem out of it."

If anyone knows for sure, it's her. She saw me with him … Hell, she may have heard me screaming his name last night. I snuck out right away, though. Asher took me around the back and drove me home, holding my hand the entire time. My right hand covers my left, right where his thumb rubbed soothing circles.

We were both quiet on the drive. He didn't say goodbye, but he did kiss me good night.

"Is this because of Asher?" Autumn asks, her green eyes curious. Renee may have evidence from the bar, and Autumn knows he dropped me off.

The two of them could piece it together easy enough.

I swallow hard. Do they know that we hooked

up in that closet, though? Were they all taking notes? This town gossips about everybody and everything. It wouldn't surprise me to find out that they've been talking about us all day. That they know how much time we spent in that storage room down to the minute.

Renee sighs, giving me a smile. "Everybody saw Asher trying to talk to you last night."

Trying to talk to me. Okay, that's good. They might not have seen us sneak off to hook up. I can't help but glance at my sister who is gazing at me, the wheels in her mind turning but her lips pressed into a firm line. She's not going to say anything … at least not right now.

Sharon, pulling her hair up into a makeshift ponytail, pipes up. "Why'd you guys break up in the first place?" Sharon's drunk, but she studies me like I'm a project for finals in college.

"They were long distance," Autumn supplies. She's quick to answer and tight lipped.

"He broke up with me." My correction is bold in the night air. That memory is one I'll never forget. Glancing down at my cup, I know I probably wouldn't tell the story like this if we weren't an hour deep into drinks. I'd be more reserved and gentler. I'm anything but when I tell them, "He said he couldn't give me what I wanted."

Sharon gives a cry of surprise and falls back into

her chair, wide eyed and dramatic, a hand up to her forehead. "He did not say that."

"Oof," Magnolia chimes in. She's had her own run-in with crazy and emotional love. Very recently in fact, so I'm not surprised that she's quiet and doing everything she can not to comment on it. In this town, it's the offhanded remarks and gossip that can break up couples and tear people down.

"Oh, he said it." I take another long sip from my plastic cup, draining it. "I'm going to need a few more drinks if I'm going to tell the whole story."

"Me too," says Sharon. She looks like she might say more. "I can't believe he would have the audacity—"

She's cut off. My sister reaches over and covers her mouth. "Hush up, lush." Sharon laughs, the sound muffled by my sister's hand until she pushes it away. Both of them crack up and Renee and Magnolia join them.

"The past is in the past," Autumn says, looking carefully at me as I stand up, my phone in hand, burning to be answered. I haven't forgotten he called me baby. Or the way his message made me feel all hopeful and raw.

"Either way," I point out, "I've got to get a refill."

Sharon groans. "You're such a tease. I want to know what happened."

"I'll be back in a minute." They're already talking and laughing about something else Sharon said the moment my back is turned. The night is still light and fun, like it should be. Even though there's this ache in my chest.

They all beg me to hurry back as I open the screen door on the patio, heading into the kitchen. If I tell everybody what happened with Asher, it's going to mean reliving it all over again. I'll never forget how he broke up with me over the freaking phone. I saw it coming, even though I didn't want to. Admitting it to myself was the most painful experience.

Things had been off between us for weeks. No, more like months. Asher was supposed to come see me, but then he canceled. Over and over. He took forever to answer my texts and my calls. Then, when he did message me, he seemed distant. I tried to tell myself that he was just busy, but I knew better.

Our friendship was too strong. I know how he sounds over text. I know how he sounds when he leaves a message. Everything was wrong. I was hurt, and I was angry. I hated how jealous I felt of everyone he was putting first.

I should have been able to talk to him about it, but he kept saying he was fine. There was nothing wrong. That I needed to stop and calm down. All I needed was for him to come see me like he said he would.

49

So when he said something came up, for the fourth time in a row … Well, I was prepared.

I knew he was going to break up with me the second I saw his name on my phone. I knew he didn't love me anymore. Something had changed.

The memory hits me hard as I lean on the granite counter and take a deep breath.

Last night wasn't about anything starting again. It wasn't about the past, or the breakup. It wasn't even love. It was lust. Lust and nothing else. It's nothing to be ashamed of. I wanted him, just like I always have.

He wanted me … that's not promising anything to give him that, right? It was a night to get over it. My fingers drift up to my throat where he kissed me. I can tell myself that at least.

Pouring another sangria, I turn to go back outside, where the laughter can be faintly heard. Instead I pace through the house in an attempt to clear my head before going back out there.

I just need a few minutes to sift through these memories. I'm quiet, so no one takes notice of me. All the kids are upstairs sleeping. My nephew Cameron is only a few months old, though, so he could wake up any minute. I'm as silent as can be with that in mind. Mags usually brings her daughter, but she got a sitter tonight for Bridget. The only rumble of any sorts comes from down the hall. The guys are in the living room with beers. It's Brody's night off from the bar. He and Griffin own it. I'm half surprised Renee isn't working tonight, given that Griffin is. The thought makes my lips perk up but then I realize something.

All of the guys are generally together, just like they are tonight. Asher's not here, though. I feel a pang. I wish he were here. That's the dumbest thing about this situation. It doesn't feel right without him.

I fan my face, letting it cool down a little more before taking another drink. I need my game face on to tell Sharon exactly what happened. Whatever I do, I'm not going to cry talking about a breakup that happened two years ago. It only takes a minute and a few more sips of liquid courage before I pull the screen door open, but when I step back outside onto the porch, it's quiet.

"Somebody's here for you, Brianna," Autumn says.

"Who?" I spent all that time getting myself together, and now I feel tipsy again. "We're all here already."

Autumn tilts her head toward the other side of the porch, and there he is. Asher.

My stomach drops. It's like he heard me thinking about him and appeared in the middle of our gathering. Is this because I didn't text him back? For a moment, I can't breathe.

In worn jeans and a black tee, he makes blue collar

look sexy as hell. Glancing at his stubble reminds me of how it rubbed against my neck last night as he fucked me against the wall.

"Hey, Asher." My voice is an octave higher than it should be. As I'm clearing my throat, he smirks.

"Bri."

They're all going to talk about this, no matter what happens. One conversation at the bar is nothing. Asher showing up here and asking for me? That's something. That's what kind of town this is. That's what kind of friends I have. They care, and they talk, and there will be an interrogation the moment Asher leaves.

I steady myself and meet his steely gaze. "What brings you here?" Everyone is staring. Everyone is waiting. If the girls could have popcorn in their laps right now, I'm sure they would. I'd hear them crunching away in the background.

He glances over my shoulder to where all the girls are gathered, then back at me. "Can we talk?" Asher slips his hands in his pockets. "Maybe inside?"

I pull myself up tall, even though my face is hot.

I open the door for him, feeling everyone's eyes on my back, and go inside. He pulls it closed behind us. My heart is racing faster than it did last night. There's a charge in the air between us. Did he come here because he couldn't stay away?

"I swear I was going to text you back …" I start.

His gaze is pinned on me as he murmurs, "That's fine."

We both know it's not.

"Is that why you came?" I ask and he shakes his head no, his gaze slipping down over my body. We were so close last night. It felt like being able to breathe again after two years underwater. I try not to feel his hands on my skin and the heat between my legs at the memories.

When he's finished looking at me, Asher takes a quick look around the kitchen. He'll be looking for anything that's out of place. Anything that needs a handyman. He must not find anything, because his eyes return to mine.

"Tell me why you came," I insist. It's too hard to stand here in the kitchen with him, struggling through the silence. "Seriously, Asher. Just tell me."

Chapter 6

Asher

I T'S BEEN A YEAR SINCE I'VE STEPPED FOOT IN this kitchen. Her mom had it redone while Bri was away last summer and it fucking killed me to be in here without her. New paint and counters and fixtures. It was mostly just a facelift, but the space looks so much better with the updates. I love being hands on, but I couldn't do it. I passed over the work to Tom and Ben. They're brothers and the two of them constantly help me out. I wouldn't have been able to get Brody and Griffin's bar done so quickly without their help.

I couldn't stop playing back every memory I had with Bri and cursing myself for letting her think I didn't want her anymore.

I saw it when it was finished, though, smiled and

shook her dad's hand. I could barely look him in the eyes. All I saw reflected back was pity.

Looking at Bri, standing in the same damn spot, all I see is uncertainty. She shifts left, then right, holding onto the counter and then crossing her arms all in the same minute. She's uncomfortable as hell. She's standing up tall, like I came here to break up with her all over again. The one thing I love about her is how she refuses to back down or cower. It was never toward me, though. "So what did you want to say?" I fucking hate this.

Guilt clenches my heart. I bet she thinks I'm going to tell her last night was a mistake. Fucking hell. Silence eats up a moment as I run my hands through my hair.

No wonder she'd think that. No wonder she'd be nervous. The way she holds it is different now. Fiercer. More confident. But that look in her eyes is something she can't hide. I know it all too well.

Just like that, I'm back in school again, wishing on everything I had to get to sit next to her in class. Hell. Just seeing her in the hallway was enough to get my heart racing. I'm being an asshole, making her wait. I just feel like I'm about to ask her to prom. Or propose.

"You want to go to Robert's after-party with me?"

A beat passes. She narrows her eyes, obviously not expecting that from me. "After-party?"

"He just got the approval for some funding for

the schools. Robert and Gary are throwing a thing to celebrate."

Brianna laughs a little, glancing down at the floor. "That funny?"

"No, it's just …" She smiles up at me. "Times are changing, huh? You used to skip school and drink. Now look at all of you."

A chuckle leaves me in a breath. That's true, I guess. I'm drawn into the warmth between us. It's so easy with us. Taking a step, I close the distance and breathe her in. Just like last night. I couldn't stop if I tried. I've wanted to be near her every second since I dropped her off last night. There's a nagging bit in my chest, an ache that wants to know why she didn't text me back. But I let it go.

"So, come with me then? To the bar tomorrow night?"

She hesitates, her grip tightening on the counter behind her. "To the bar tomorrow night?" she repeats back and I smirk at her, running my thumb over my bottom lip before taking another step closer and teasing her. "That's what I said."

Heat blisters between us as she stares back wordlessly and then her gaze drops to my mouth.

Our lips are an inch apart when Bri pulls away.

I'm hot all over, pain going through my chest. What the hell's happening?

"Are you all right?" I ask. Clearly she's not. If everything was okay, she'd have kissed me. All the heat from my body disappears.

Bri shifts against the countertop, putting a little space between us, looking as uncomfortable as I've ever seen her. "I don't know." I take the hint and take a step back as well. Giving her space, but not leaving.

"Is everything okay with last night, Bri?" It's another question I already know the answer to. She hasn't been texting me back.

"Yeah," she answers quickly but also like she's shrugging off the question.

I nod without agreeing. More like I'm acknowledging she just lied to me. "Are you okay with me being here now?"

Brianna hesitates, and even though her hesitation hurts my heart, she's beautiful. Her long dark hair. Those gorgeous green eyes. That mouth of hers. I've never been able to take my eyes off her. She was my best friend. And she's not okay with last night. I should have known.

Fuck, fuck, fuck.

I run my hands through my hair, gritting my teeth trying to figure out how I can fix this. I think about walking out the back door and disappearing. It'll be obvious. All the girls are sitting out there. We're both trapped in this kitchen until we figure something out. A second ago, it was spacious and welcoming. Now it's fencing us in.

"Asher," Bri says, biting her lip. I hate what she's going to say before she has a chance to say it. "I think it would be a mistake to get back together."

My entire body goes cold. No. No, take it back. Denial hits me, then remorse. I fucked it up. Every thought tries to ram its way out of my mouth, but I'm silent, needing to be careful. Needing to make sure I play this right.

I knew it was coming, but it still hits me like a punch to the chest. A mistake to get back together. A mistake. "What was last night, then?" I question and I can't stop it from coming, the hurt wrapping around my insides.

I'm not ready for the answer Brianna gives me. A mistake.

I can't speak. I can't answer. I can barely stand upright.

Before I know it, I'm walking out of the front door with Briana calling after me. I can't stop, though. I don't even look back.

Four hours later, I'm staring at the ceiling over my bed. The dim light from the digital display of my alarm clock makes for poor company.

I'm exhausted, but I can't fall asleep. All I can think about is that conversation with Brianna. It felt like she was telling me we were a mistake in the first place. She'd be right. I'd never have had to hurt her if I'd never wanted her. I did it anyway.

The floors creak somewhere outside my bedroom door. Either my mom or my dad is moving around in the kitchen. I'm half listening when my phone lights up with a text.

Brianna: *Please don't hate me.*

A chill runs through my body. I've lain here since I got home. Trying to think, but nothing in my head is helpful. It's filled with every time I let her down and the moments I could go back to in order to make things right.

She texts again: *Can we just be friends?*

The message hits me harder than it should. I don't know if she's suggesting it because that's what I told her when we broke up, or because she genuinely means it. I don't know if she's throwing it in my face or really wants to be friends.

Dropping the phone to my bed, I cut out all of the uncertainty.

Hell, of course I know. Bri's never spiteful. She gets mad. We all do. But she wouldn't text me anything to be sarcastic or mean. That's not her.

The front door to the house opens and closes, the sound earning my attention. I sit up in bed and listen to the shuffling out in the driveway. The mattress groans under me as I peek out through the window.

My dad's out there.

My stomach churns. It only takes a moment to realize there's no reason to be nervous. He's got a bag of trash dangling from his hand before tossing it in the bin. Dad's been sober for almost two years, but I'm on edge anyway. He used to leave to go get booze at the corner store. Him leaving in the middle of the night was one of the first signs.

He lets the top slam shut to the bin. The night goes still around him. Crickets stop chirping and then they start right back up. They don't mind. Nothing's wrong out there.

I'm the only one who worries that there's another problem coming, and soon. Me and my mother.

My dad heads back toward the house, and I lie back

down. We live in the backwoods and always have. This house was my grandfather's. It's tucked away from the town and nobody would see how drunk my dad would get. That was a plus. My mother said she was grateful for that reprieve. At the same time, he had to walk to the liquor store if he wanted more booze. It was dangerous as hell. He could have been arrested. He could have gotten hit by a car, stumbling across the road. Thank God he never did.

I don't relax completely until the front door shuts and I hear him flip the deadbolt.

My phone pings again and it's Bri: *I know I have no right, but I do want to be friends with you. I think I need that first, Asher.*

First. That single word has all kinds of hope in it. Then what? When she knows I'm still the man who wants to be her best friend, then what's next?

I text her back: *You promise we can be friends? That's all you want to be right now.*

Bri: *I'll admit I miss you. Please, can we start there?*

A breath comes and goes. It's not easy, but it's easier than it was. If there's one thing I know, it's that Brianna's going to have a hold on me for the rest of my life. No matter what happens. If she's asking me to be friends, then I'm more than happy to start there.

Asher: *Yeah, Bri.*

I almost add that I love her. That I've loved her for forever. From the first time I heard her laugh. But I don't. I settle back onto my pillow and type out another text.

Asher: *Can I see you tomorrow? Or is that too much?*

Bri: *Yeah. I'd really like to see you. I wish you hadn't left earlier.*

I hesitate to respond and her next text comes before I can.

Bri: *I'm working, but then maybe we can get takeout and catch up?*

One simple question, and it brings back so many memories of sitting on the couch together. We were too broke for restaurants, but to-go bags and a bench did just fine.

That was our thing. We'd get food from this place or that place, find a spot to sit side by side, and talk. Those were our best dates. I almost ask her if she remembers them too. I almost ask her if they make her chest all warm in the middle when she thinks about them. Those times with Brianna are where my mind wanders when I have a bad day. I just picture myself sitting on a bench somewhere, takeout in our laps, laughing.

There are a million things I could say, but I don't want to push her too far. I've done that enough tonight. It was proof that I fucked up worse than I thought. I knew the breakup had hurt her. I just didn't think she'd chalk it up to a mistake.

Craziest part is, now that she's texting me, I'm hopeful. We were friends once. If Brianna wants to start as friends again, then there's a chance.

"Don't get too far ahead of yourself," I say out loud. I shouldn't even be thinking about it. It's not fair to her after what I did, and after what I'm still not telling her.

My fingers hover over the screen of my phone. I have the urge to spill my secrets now. Tell her everything. Big blocks of text on the screen. All the justifications I made to myself, and how scared I was, and how I wanted to call her and ask her to come home. How I needed her but at the same time, I couldn't. She was living her dream and I wanted to be there, but I was barely holding on.

I just couldn't. I couldn't let her see what was happening to my dad. I couldn't let her see what was happening to me. I think if she knew, she wouldn't think last night was a mistake. She'd know us breaking up was.

I don't want her to think I'm telling her as a way to get close, though. I desperately want to be close to her, but not like this.

It's fine and she doesn't need to know, I remind myself. Dad's not drinking. He took the garbage out and came back. He didn't go walking down the road in the middle of the night to get drunk. It's all okay. All is right for the moment.

Bri's waiting for an answer.

Asher: *Of course we can. You pick a place. Wherever you want. I'll be waiting for you when you get out of work.*

Chapter 7

Brianna

THERE HAVE BEEN VERY FEW CHANGES TO MY parents' real estate office since I was a child. There are new chairs. A new coat of paint on the walls, but it's the same soothing shade of pale mauve. There's a new plaque on the wall behind my mother's desk, though. It's an award for being one of the top realtors in the region. Staring at it makes me smile, knowing my name is carved under her desk where I used to hide makes me smirk.

Maybe it makes me a little sappy, but I'm proud of my parents every time I walk in here. I'm not sure if it's where I'll stay and what I want my career to be, but it's comforting that I have this job and I get to work with them while I find my way. It's a good job to boot, even if it mostly has to do with paperwork.

Between this job and the salon, I have my old life back but times ten in a way.

Growing up, I was in the office all the time. My dad stayed home with me when I was very young, and more often than not, he was the one dropping me off and picking me up from school. He was a realtor, too, but my mom was the one who was always out and about.

Technically, it's my father's business. But in reality, she's the one who's one of the top realtors in the region for selling vacation homes.

Dropping the stack of printouts on my mom's desk in her empty office, I leave it behind to return to my desk, which is plain and waiting for a cute mug full of colorful pens, frames I bought last week that still need to be filled with pictures from back in college, and other personal touches. Right now the only pop of color is a stack of yellow Post-It notes and the only way anyone knows it's mine is from the paper sign that says "Brianna Holloway." Settling into my chair, everything that I still have to do piles up in my mental to-do list, but it's swept away quickly, just like everything else has all morning.

Because I can't stop thinking about Asher.

The other night took me back to the way things used to be between us. It was a flash of a moment and the escape was everything I could have dreamed of. Heck, I have dreamed of that moment. The two of us forgetting about everything that's happened and just loving on each other. I seek refuge in my cup of coffee, blowing on top of it only to take a sip and realize it's room temperature now. My head falls back and I try to snap myself out of it for the tenth time today.

I don't know what I was thinking.

An escape is one thing. A moment of passion. Real life is another.

My gaze shifts to my phone and my sister's text about lunch. There are none from him waiting for me to read and I haven't sent him any either. It's not like this is a conversation we can have over text, or even standing around in the kitchen. It's probably a talk that will take a decent amount of time. So I can trust him again. A lump forms in my throat and the lukewarm coffee is barely enough to get rid of it.

I considered texting him a hundred times last night. Typing things like: *What are you thinking? What happened? Why did you break up with me? What did I do that was too much for you?*

I know I did something. That's the only explanation that makes any sense for what happened between us. I know it was my fault but I think I'd do it again, and I don't even know what it was. That's the root of it all and I so desperately want to message him and ask. I was insecure, I know that much and it felt like every time I opened my mouth, I made it seem like I was questioning us. That's not what I meant to do. I just … I needed more of him. Maybe that's what it was? I was too needy?

I could ask, but Asher wants to move past all that.

Jumping in headfirst would be reckless. It hurt too much to say goodbye the first time. The bottom line is, I don't trust him. I haven't trusted any man since he threw me away like he did.

Stretching first, I lean forward in my chair and try to focus harder on the paperwork.

The effort lasts a whole thirty seconds since the next document on my list is Asher's parents' house. They're moving?

I stop and scroll back up, scanning through the paperwork.

"The Hart house is going up for sale?" I shoot a glance at my mom just as she walks in, drops her purse on her desk and takes her seat. With my mouth still open in question.

"What was that, Bri?" she asks, slipping off her mint green cardigan that gives her tweed cream dress a very uptown feel and settling into her seat.

My butt is out of my seat in a flash, paper in hand.

She's been a machine all morning. A brilliant, cheery machine. Call after call, never getting impatient. She's a powerhouse. And now is the perfect time for a break … so I can dig for information. "Isn't this Asher's house?"

"His parents' house, technically." She flashes me a smile over a file folder in her hands. Information not forthcoming at all. *Come on, Mom.* I wait a moment, but no other information comes. She does peer up at me, though, a single brow raised expectantly.

"Asher didn't tell me that."

My mom hums and considers me. "Is it something you think he would or should tell you?"

I hesitate.

"Is that the …" She pauses to reach into her purse for her phone and a tube of lip balm before rephrasing her question. "Are you two talking like that again?"

I know she's asking because she wants more information. My mom talks to just about everybody in town most days. She'll have heard things about me and Asher. Of course she knew about the breakup before anyone else. I texted her that night. Same with my sister. This particular situation that just happened in the back of the bar, though … that's not something I want my mother to be aware of. I wonder if I'm reading regular curiosity into her tone or … hope.

"No," I answer with a hard swallow. "I guess not."

"It would be if the two of you were back together." My mom switches out a couple of folders. "Are you?"

"No." I let out a surprised laugh, my face heating up. "No, we're definitely not together."

"Huh," she says. It's an invitation to keep talking. That light little noise could mean anything, coming from her. That she's surprised we're not together or that she thinks it'll happen or … nothing at all.

It's hard to resist the temptation to share. I nearly pull the chair back behind me rather than stay standing. I could tell my mother anything. Shifting the weight from one foot to the other, I give her a little info.

"I'm going to see him tonight, though." It's the truth. There's also no need to hide it from my mom. If Asher and I start spending time together, she'll know about it anyway. In a town like this, it's best to be ahead of the gossip.

"Oh, really?" I honestly can't tell if she's pretending to be deeply into her work or what. "By the way, did you get those comps over to Mary?"

"Almost done with them," I say. "I'm just wrapping up the contracts for Jason first."

"Sounds good." Mom faces her computer screen and scrolls, her fingers deft on her mouse. Asher's parents' place flashes up on her screen. "This house," she murmurs, almost to herself. "It needs work done, but the market's hot for the area. Easy to sell. They'd probably tear it down, though."

The thought of Asher's house being torn down brings a lump to my throat. I swallow back my emotions. It's not because I'm still in love with him. It's because I've known his house for years. A realtor like my mom would see that it needs work, but all I can see is all the happy memories that exist there. I'd rather put the work in than see it reduced to rubble.

I can't imagine this town without him and his family. His dad has this gut laugh that makes everyone else around him laugh too. And his mom was the one who did all the decor for every school play. They're a part of this town and I don't understand why they would move.

It kills me to think I don't know everything about Asher anymore. We used to be so close. Close enough, I thought, to overcome any problems that came our way. That's why, even though I saw it coming, the breakup still blindsided me in the end. I truly believed we'd be able to push past whatever was happening in our lives. If I could make time for him at school, he could make time for me back in town.

"Everything okay, Bri?" Mom asks.

"Yeah, fine," I answer softly, then clear my throat. "Of course," I answer with more conviction.

"You could tell me anything if you wanted, you know?" My mom attempts to remain casual but I see right through it. She's worried for me.

"I'm totally fine," I answer her for the third time, but this time is more convincing.

"Good, good," she answers and then returns to her computer.

I sneak a glance at her while she's studying her screen. My mom looks older than I usually picture her. I know, obviously, that my mom is older than she was when I left for college, but I guess I didn't realize how quickly time was passing until I came back to town. The last four years seemed to happen in the blink of an eye. The breakup with Asher feels like it was seconds ago, not two years. There are soft wrinkles around her eyes and grays are peeking out from her dyed hair. The women in my family all look alike, my sister included.

I nearly turn around and head back to my seat, but my phone lights up with a text in my hand and my body freezes.

Asher: *Hey, about tonight.*

My heart races thinking he's going to bail.

"Is that him?" My mother's voice is calm and knowing. All I can do is nod and then she clarifies, "It's Asher?"

"How did you know?" I ask.

She smiles at me, knowing, and for a moment she looks just the way I remember her from my childhood days. "Because I know you, baby girl." My mom rises from her seat and walks past, gently slapping her file folder against the back of my head. Then she leans down to kiss my forehead.

"Mom, I'm working," I grumble in a joking way. "That's, like, harassment or something."

My mom laughs, delighted at my joke, but leaves me be. Even though I'm the one intruding since this is her office.

I text him back: *Are you still able to make it?*

I'm very much wrong about him canceling. It's something else entirely: *My mom asked if you wanted to come for dinner.*

With my brow raised, I slowly make my way back to my desk. It's not until I've lowered myself into the chair that I'm able to process it.

That house was practically my second home. His mother was like my second mother. Then it was shut down cold turkey. I haven't heard a word from either of them since Asher broke up with me. Not that we talked regularly. It was only really when I was over his house before. Which was anytime we weren't at my own house.

Everything is different now, though. It would be our first dinner at his house since the breakup.

I answer with my gut instinct, although I feel nothing but anxious about it: *Sure. I'll bring a bottle of wine!*

Asher starts to type, then stops. He starts again. Stops.

There's a long pause.

I sit forward in my seat, eyes glued to the phone waiting. It's so strange. He's usually quick with his replies and doesn't need a lot of time to think. I scroll back to figure out if I've said something wrong. I don't think I did. He was clearly hurt during our conversation last night, but we went ahead with our plans.

It takes three more minutes for his answer to come.

Asher: *I'm looking forward to it.* I don't understand why it took that long to answer and just the fact that I am reading so much into this and overthinking everything makes me second-guess everything.

Chapter 8

Asher

I'M ANXIOUS AS ALL HELL AS I OPEN THE DOOR, but the sight of her numbs all of that. She's always been able to do that to me. I don't know how. It's just when she's smiling at me, even if it's a nervous one as she holds out a bottle of wine, everything's going to be all right. I just know it will be.

"Hey there," I say and almost add "cutie" as I take the wine from her. The bottle is heavy; it's a red but I don't check to see what kind it is. I have to bite my lip from telling her she looks cute as hell.

"Hey there yourself," she says and a blush creeps up her cheeks. I fucking love it. She's still into me. She can't deny that. "Are you going to let me in?" she jokes with a feminine laugh and I step aside, widening the door for her to enter.

Her hair sways as she walks in, all done in shiny waves. It reminds me of before. All of this feels like it was before.

I have to stop thinking of "before." I have to stop thinking of how it was. I just can't help it. Bri belongs in this house just like I do. She belongs by my side. The second she's inside the foyer, my shoulders relax.

She goes on tiptoes to kiss my cheek. The moment she does, I think she second-guesses it. "Sorry," she tells me, "bad habit I guess." I think I'll feel that touch forever, but I try to play it cool. "It's fine," I say, shrugging it off and change the subject, ignoring the warring emotions that make me anxious for tonight. "I'm glad you still wanted to come."

"Of course I did."

"Mom's in the kitchen. Dad's upstairs."

She heads to the kitchen without waiting for me as I close the door behind me with a smile that won't quit. Does she mess me up inside? Yeah. But does she make it feel like not a damn thing matters but being with her? Also yeah.

Plus, she couldn't help but kiss me.

"Brianna! My Bri," I hear my mother say before I step inside the threshold to the kitchen, slipping my hand into my pocket.

My mom's face is lit up and it's been a while since

I've seen her smile like that. "Honey, hi," she says again, embracing Bri a little too tight and a little too long before holding her at arm's length. "We're so glad to see you. How are things at your mom's place?"

"Great," Bri says and as she does, my mom sees the bottle in my hands. I place it on the counter as a frown forms on my mother's face. Bri's statement takes her attention once again and my mom's quick to correct her fallen expression before Bri can see. "Oh my gosh, let me help you. What can I do?"

My mom tries to insist she's fine, but Bri won't take no for an answer. Within minutes they're chatting near the stove, stepping around each other to put the finishing touches on dinner. The savory scent of seasoned potatoes and baked chicken fills the room. Mom said it's Bri's favorite. She insisted it was.

Judging by how wide Bri's green eyes get when she sees the platter, I'm going to have to agree.

"What should I carry in first?" asks Bri, practically salivating. It's just like old times. I can't help but keep thinking about it.

The dinner table is already set. It's simple with a vase of sunflowers in the middle. Bri's comfortable around my mom. It brings up more than a few emotions to see the ease between them. Bri and my mom go back and forth to the dining room table, and then my mom calls for my dad.

We're taking our seats when he comes into the dining room, looking a little worn out but smiling nonetheless. "Bri," he says. "Nice to see you." His overalls have a smudge on them from the garage and I know he'll be back there tonight.

"It's so good to see you too." Bri's smile is genuine. My nerves amp up, but then they retreat. "Dig in," my dad tells her.

Bri doesn't hesitate and the chicken is the first thing she piles onto her plate. Mom has the green beans, which she then passes to Dad. I scoop out the potatoes and realize my mom went overboard.

"We can't eat all of this, Mom," I say over the clinking of utensils. "There's so much food."

My mom flushes, and she waves me off. "I wanted there to be plenty for everybody."

"You did just right," my dad says and he and Mom share a glance with a soft smile. Dishes are handed around the table.

"So, Brianna, what are you up to? You back home for good now?" my father asks. "Tell us everything."

"Well," Bri says, her face lighting up. "You know I'm working at my mom's office. Just for the time being and the salon on the weekends. I'm not really sure what I'm doing with my degree but I'm happy I have it."

"Oh! The salon?" My mom practically applauds in excitement. "I'll have to make an appointment with you."

"I don't want to steal you away from your stylist," Bri says.

"I've been looking for somebody new. You're perfect." A huff of a laugh leaves me. My mom is laying it on thick. It's making Bri smile, though.

The two of them carry on, laughing and chatting.

It's a joyful sound. The kind of sound that belongs in this house. The kind that's been gone for too long.

My dad's quiet for most of the conversation and so am I. We shovel food in and answer questions when asked as the two of them catch up. He's always been a quiet man. The loudest he gets is when he's drunk. I'm glad he's not a chatterbox tonight. I'd be worried as hell if he was.

"Oh, I forgot the salad dressing in the kitchen," Bri says. "I meant to bring it out."

"I'll get it." I get up out of my seat, the chair legs grinding against the wooden floor, glad for the chance to catch my breath. Having her here, even if it is as just a friend, is a little too good to be true. It's like any moment something could happen and it will all fall apart. I wish I could shake the feeling but I can't.

My mom asks another question as I head into the kitchen. I lean against the counter, breathing deep. The Italian dressing is out waiting on the counter. It's Bri's preference but no one else here eats it so the bottle is brand new.

Footsteps behind me get my attention.

Dad pats my shoulder. "You doing okay?"

"Course I am." I straighten up, grabbing the dressing. "Just taking a breather."

"Those two love to talk," he says affectionately, and with a huff of a laugh. "Hard to keep up with all the developments."

"I don't mind sitting back and letting them have at it." I lean against the counter. Dad's off. Maybe he's anxious too. Maybe he feels guilty like I do. Maybe I'm just imagining it.

He looks out the window over the sink, into the backyard. "When you leave," he says quietly, "I want you to take that bottle with you." His gaze shifts to the wine but I keep my eyes on him.

"You got it." I was already planning to take it with us. I glance back toward the dining room. Mom and Bri's voices make their way down the hall to us. "I didn't tell her anything." I clear my throat before asking him, "Do you think I should?"

He thinks about it for a minute, his gaze assessing me. "I don't think your mom would like that." His tone holds regret. Yeah, he's feeling what I'm feeling. Or something like it. This weight against my chest. I hate it. "We don't need anybody else talking about it. It would make things harder for her at work, and I don't want that. Don't let Bri know. Okay?" It's not hard to see he's worried about Bri taking offense to them not opening it.

"Yeah. She doesn't need to know."

"I just don't want her to think we're ungrateful if we don't drink the wine."

In an attempt to put him at ease I tell him, "She won't even notice. I think she's happy to just be here, and I'll take care of it."

My dad's brow wrinkles. He really is worried about what Bri might think. If they're going to hurt her feelings by not drinking the wine. And I'm sure he doesn't want word to get around town. The only way to keep a secret in a place like this is to keep your mouth closed, even when you want to talk.

"Let's get back there before they forget about us." My father laughs at my joke and we walk back in. I haven't even scooted my chair in before the front door bangs open.

"Hello?"

"We're in here, Robert," my mother calls casually and Robert's already in the threshold before I can turn around, his hand around the tie he's wearing. No jacket and his dress shirt sleeves rolled up to his elbows. I bet he's on his way to the after-party.

His eyebrows go up at the sight of us sitting around the table. "I didn't realize I was interrupting."

"You're never interrupting," my dad says, waving him off and then picking his fork back up.

"Speak for yourself. This man's a menace," I joke. By menace, I mean my best friend and the closest thing I've ever had to a brother.

Robert laughs behind me and I invite him to sit down and eat, but he shakes his head before turning to Bri.

"Good to see you, Bri," Robert says. He comes farther into the room. "I just came over to drop off the keys Missy said you needed, Ash."

Bri's eyebrows go up, and Robert smirks.

"Missy's car is in the shop," I explain, a hand over my mouth, before I can even swallow my potato and I nearly choke on it.

"That's what you get for speaking with your mouth full," my mother says under her breath.

I don't turn to look at her, though, I keep my eyes on Bri who shakes off whatever came over her at the mention of Missy.

Bri shrugs like she's not bothered and there's no need for an explanation, but I catch her glancing down at her plate. She's clearly feeling something. If she's jealous, that's a good sign. It means she can't deny that there's something between us. We fit so well together. Bri thought so the other night at the bar. I know it because I felt it too. It was like coming home after a long time away. I almost tell her Missy's husband dropped off the car, but I'm cut off.

"Ash, did you hear me?"

"What?" I ask.

Everybody laughs. Bri blushes. I've been staring at her, thinking about her without realizing.

"Where do you want me to leave the keys?" Robert asks.

"Counter's fine. I'll get them after we're done."

"All right, you got it," Robert says and heads toward the door, but turns on his heel and trots back over. "So … you two." He points between me and Bri.

"We're playing things by ear tonight," I tell him but he shakes his head.

"I'm asking," he says, then gestures between us and repeats, "you two?"

An asymmetric smirk finds itself on my face as I toss my napkin at him.

"Are friends." I cut him off before he can say any more. Bri nods, agreeing with me. My smile doesn't leave, though, as she glances at me.

"I just got home," she says with a smile and then nervously glances at me. "Still settling in." I like that she looks to me for reassurance. Hell, I like that she looks to me at all.

Just friends doesn't seem right, but if it's what she wants right now, I ... am trying to let her lie to herself.

Robert grins back. "Well, Asher's not the only one who's glad you're home. We're all glad you're back, Bri."

"Thanks," she answers and the two of them half hug while she's still seated.

With a tap on the doorway, Robert leaves, and there's a lull in our conversation.

"Does anyone want a glass of wine?" Bri asks.

"Oh, no thank you," my mother answers. My dad shakes his head. They're polite. Smiling. Bri looks between them and smiles too.

"Just thought I'd ask. Dinner was wonderful. So good."

My dad is visibly relieved when Bri doesn't insist or get up to get herself a glass. Before another moment passes, I ask Bri, "You want to go out tonight?"

She looks at me in surprise. "Out? Me and you?" My pulse quickens and I can feel my parents staring at us. She can't say no with them watching, though.

"Yeah, we can go hang out with whoever's at the bar."

Bri laughs, hesitating.

"You don't have to go if you don't want to. You could just sit here with my parents all night."

"Asher!" she exclaims, then shakes her head at my mom. "I wouldn't mind hanging out with you guys. I hope you know that."

"I certainly do." My mom beams with a kind smile. I think she's happy Bri and she still have that mutual fondness even after two years of radio silence. "You two should head out," she says, urging Bri. Great, my mom is now my wingman.

"I'll help you with the dishes," Bri offers.

"No thank you." My mom puts up her hand. "The two of you should go have some fun. Where do you think you'll go?"

"Everybody's going to be at the bar tonight for Robert's after-party. I figured we'd head there."

Bri nods along, already agreeing.

"Then go," my mom says, waving us away. "The night's not getting any younger. We'll handle things here."

And with that I stand, offering a hand to Bri to help her up. Just friends, I have to remind myself that's what we're supposed to be right now. Just friends.

My mom follows us to the foyer. "Come anytime you want for dinner," she says, giving Bri a hug.

"Dinner was delicious," Bri insists again. "Thank you. It was really good to see all of you."

"Go have fun." My mom shoos us out of the house, and it's even better to help Bri into her car. She drove here, so we're driving separately.

The moment the car door closes it's less anxious, easier. It's how it used to be. She's smiling as she buckles her seat belt.

"What's that grin for?"

She shrugs. "I had fun. It was nice, Asher. I'm glad you invited me."

The engine comes to life as she turns the ignition, the window rolled down so I can lean in some. "I'm glad you didn't mind the change of plans."

"Me too. I missed you and your family," she admits and there's a hint of nostalgia in her tone. She feels this too. She has to be feeling this too.

That urge comes back again. I want to tell her everything. I want to break down and let go of this secret I've been hiding from her. That would only ruin the evening. I've invited Bri out, and that's what we're going to do. Go out. Have fun. Be friends.

Friends, and nothing else.

"Meet you at the bar … *friend*," she teases. That was her teasing me, right?

Chapter 9

Brianna

I can't help but smile as I take a sip of cabernet. Sitting at the bar feels like home. The whole town does, actually. The people, the smells, every little thing. Asher's house. My parents' house. These are the places I know the best. They welcome me back like I never left. I could almost believe I hadn't, especially here.

The billiard balls clack together as they're being racked behind me, and someone laughs in the corner of the bar. All the while there's the din of conversation and cheering in time with the football game on the television. The fried pickles are salty and the dip has a touch of spice; the local beer is cold and hoppy. Even though this bar is brand new, straight from the studs, it still feels like home. Probably because of the people in it. This is what home is to me.

The pool table has a handful of guys from out of town gathering around it. They probably go to the university a bit aways judging by their age. Older men are grouped together, forming huddles in the opposite corner. They're my friends' uncles or former teachers. Aside from the newcomers, everybody's a familiar face.

At the pool table, the out-of-towners are going up against a guy we knew in high school. He likes to think he's a shark, but he's getting his ass kicked. And he loves it. He's grinning all through the game. I bet he'll blame his losses on the booze when all is said and done and be at it again, grin and all, tomorrow.

Sharon had to go to the bathroom, so I'm left standing, people watching as I sip my wine. It's not until Asher brushes past behind me, his hand grazing along my lower back that I'm brought back to the push and pull of what we are and what we've always been. Heat rushes to my face and some down below too if I'm honest. His touch is everything I've missed and everything I've needed. Scooting to the side, I hide my small gasp in another sip and pretend like I'm just fine. Like that small touch didn't do damage to the walls I pretend I've built up to keep him out. I'm so screwed. One touch has me hot and bothered. I guess that's the same as it always has been too. He's always made me feel this way.

Clearing my throat and avoiding his gaze that I can feel burning into the side of my face, I concentrate on our friends instead. Renee's keeping an eye on the room, a beer on the table in front of her. She got done with her shift a while ago, but she's still here. It's practically home for her too.

Griffin, the co-owner of the bar, is quiet and watchful. Except he's not watching the rest of the bar. He's watching Renee. It's obvious there's something between them.

Yep. I was right. As I take another sip, I watch Griffin lean in and whisper into her ear. He's a little too close for a boss-employee relationship and she's a little too comfortable. Renee cracks a smile, laughing like he told her a private joke. Maybe she stays here to spend more time with Griffin. With a clack, a plate hits the table and my attention is drawn to a salty fried food delight.

Asher slides a new plate of fried pickles down onto the table, then nudges me with his elbow. "You want one?"

I can't help but return his smile and nod.

"One more." I've already eaten half a plate. They're my favorite. The one he hands me is gone in a single bite. Maybe I'll have another too. It seems I'm addicted to all things Asher hands me. I almost tell him that. I almost flirt and brush up against him like he did me. Instead I set my wine down and wipe my fingers off on the napkin. "Who's in the kitchen? I thought it was closed already."

"Kitchen's open until eleven tonight for Rob," Griffin calls from the other side of the table with another grin. The light reflects off of the lenses of his black, plastic-framed glasses.

He's something that's changed. He's a Southerner like us, but he's new to this town. He's friendly enough. He means well. But he's definitely not from here. Nobody calls Robert "Rob." Renee's giving him a funny look, like she thinks he should know better but she likes him anyway.

Renee's never actually left home. This small town is all she knows. She's born and raised here and proudly boasts that she'll retire in a small house on the water. She never wants to leave and I don't blame her, but I'll be dragging her to as many vacation spots around the world as I can.

She nudges Griffin and this time it's him leaning down so she can whisper in his ear.

In a bar filled with similar Southern accents, Griffin's is a little muddy—almost like he spent too much time up north. That's how he met Brody; they're old college buddies who studied and partied together at the University of Delaware. I heard Brody's from somewhere in Jersey or Pennsylvania. Maybe that's what Renee likes about Griffin. He's new to her. That means he hasn't spent years following along with the gossip. He's probably got a fresh perspective.

"You're people watching," Asher murmurs, and I jump, realizing how close he is. How close he stayed since he put down that plate of pickles. A nervous laugh leaves me and I pretend there aren't butterflies fluttering in the pit of my stomach. Somehow, after dinner with his parents, he's even more handsome. More rugged. More like the man I used to dream of every single night.

"No, I'm not." I sip my drink.

Asher gives me a knowing smirk. "Don't lie to me, Bri. I know you were people watching. But I think there's something else too."

His tone is teasing and I mirror his smirk, playing along. "Something else … Like what? Drinking?"

"Like standing here all cute, pretending you don't want to go somewhere and talk."

I roll my eyes. "I know what that means." My pulse races.

"It means we didn't get to talk at dinner, and you still want to."

Damn. He's right.

"Don't be bad," he says, his voice lower now.

"Bad?"

"You know what I mean," Asher says more evenly, denying the flirtatiousness between us. "I want a real conversation, Bri. I can take you home."

"I don't know about that." The thought of going back with him sends a flurry of nerves all through me.

"You've been drinking and I'm now your designated driver."

"Oh, no you are not."

"Hmm. I feel like … that's not something you would say to a friend," he counters.

"What would I say, then?" I challenge and suddenly he leans in close, so damn close I could kiss him. Tension singes the air between us. The bar is hotter, all of a sudden.

What I should say is no. I should put that wall up between us and insist we take this slow. Friends first, so I know I can trust him again. Taking our time so I know where I went wrong. I'm the one who wanted friendship, after all. Standing next to him like this makes all those plans disappear. "No. I'm not going to do it." Emotions war inside of me at just the thought of giving him my heart again. It wouldn't take much for him to just take it at this point.

"What if I beg?" he questions.

I give a huff and a shake of my head at his ridiculousness before downing the rest of my wine.

"I would do it," he insists.

"No you wouldn't," I'm quick to reply.

It's another dare. Asher looks me in the eye and goes down to his knees, right there on the floor. My bottom lip drops and a fire breaks out along my skin.

A couple of onlookers nearby laugh. It's too close to a proposal for comfort. He's obviously being funny, but people are going to talk. People are going to notice this.

"What are you doing?" I practically hiss, setting my now empty glass down.

He looks up at me with that charming smile and puppy dog gaze, and I can hardly breathe. This is the Asher I always wanted. The one who'd beg me to stay with him for the rest of his life rather than going cold and distant. The one who'd have come to me instead of telling me it was over.

This is what I always wanted.

"If you won't let me be your boyfriend, would you please let me be your DD?" he jokes.

Or else it's the alcohol and the bar and all the good feelings from dinner.

"Get up," I urge him. "Come on, Asher. Get up."

He looks me dead in the eye. "You think I won't

show this whole damn town the woman who has me on my knees?"

A slow grin slides over his face. My body heats, then gets cold. "You have to get up." It's too serious, that tone he just gave me. That's not joking about driving me home.

I glance around. I thought they were all watching, but most of our friends are wrapped up in each other. Renee and Griffin are gazing into each other's eyes. There are a bunch of separate conversations going on. If they're talking about us, they're doing it so we can't hear. Maybe that's better.

Asher doesn't get up. He's the one challenging me now. This is more than a dare. He stays where he is and arches an eyebrow. The longer he stays down there, the more people are going to talk. He has to get up. But he's not going to do that unless I give him a real answer.

He's right. If we were friends the way we used to be, I wouldn't refuse to go anywhere with him. That's just not how we were.

"Get up, please." He has to hear the change in my voice, the desperation for him to stop laying it on thick. I'm too close to falling for him. Too close to saying yes to all sorts of things. He partially stands, but he's still leaned over in a begging position. Asher's voice turns a bit more serious, although it's still effortlessly sexy.

"Everybody's been drinking. I haven't. Let me give you a ride."

"I've had one glass," I insist, but there's a shift between us.

Something prickles in the back of my mind. Something about that bottle of wine no one would drink at dinner. He hasn't touched a sip all night. I didn't hear anybody talking about him being the DD, but they must have planned it. At the very least, people assume he's not drinking. Why?

Or did I just miss it?

I look into Asher's eyes. No. He really hasn't had anything to drink. If there's any flush to his skin, it's from this conversation and nothing else.

"I can be a polite friend. I promise," he says. "I can be a gentleman, if that's what you want. I'll take you home."

He's a good liar, because part of it's true. Asher can be a good friend. The best one. That's why everybody loves him. He's always kind and helpful. Generous. Handsome. Everybody's favorite ... and the worst kind of person to lose. How can you stop thinking about him after he's gone? How can you forget how his body felt against yours? How can you forget his hands?

I thought about calling him every time something went wrong for two years. I wanted to do it. I ached to do it.

"If we walk out of here tonight, people are really going to gossip."

He shrugs. "Let them. I'm giving you a ride home. I'm being a gentleman, and you're being …" He searches for the word. "Stubborn."

"Wow," I say, pretending to be offended. "I can't turn that down. Will you please get up now?"

"Yes."

Asher gets to his feet with a smirk, and I can't help basking in how handsome he is. It's made more powerful by the warmth of the bar. All our friends are here. Everybody's okay. There's no pressure. If I really wanted to refuse him, I could. There would be more gossip, of course. They'd watch us even more carefully, wanting to know how our story ends.

"You made me spend just about forever down there, Bri." He grins to let me know it's okay.

That grin. It's the most unforgettable thing about him. Asher's always letting me know it's okay … except when it's not. Except for the time he ended it.

I know I'm going to be thinking about this for days, but it doesn't matter. I'll think about him anyway. When I get up in the morning. When I go to bed. Sometimes, it's better to just accept your fate.

My fate doesn't seem so bad right about now.

"Don't complain," I say jokingly. "You got what you wanted. Now take me home."

"One quick question," he adds as I reach for my purse.

"What's that?"

"Do you want me to be a gentleman?" he asks.

I pat his chest, which is harder than I remember, very much knowing what he's asking and I tease him, "As if you could be a perfect gentleman."

He half laughs and then he takes my hand in his. "If you'd rather Renee take you home, I'm pretty sure she's waiting and wouldn't mind. Then you wouldn't have to worry about my ulterior motives."

"Ulterior motives? Don't tell me you have those."

"Fine then, Bri baby," he says and grins, taking his keys from his pocket. "I'll keep them a secret."

Ulterior motives.

"Just friends, right?" I question him.

"How do you feel about friends with benefits?" he asks.

"Maybe," I answer and step in front of him to lead the way. So many questions are racing through my mind.

He gets to the bar door first, though, opening it for me and letting the cool evening air wrap around us. "I'll take a maybe. I can work with that."

Chapter 10

Asher

WITH HER HEAD LAID BACK, SWAYING gently to the country song on the radio, Bri looks perfect, right where she's meant to be. Everything feels just right. Friends or lovers, whatever it is in this moment. I know that it's just right.

I drive her home on the roads I've known all my life. There's a fork up ahead. One branch goes back toward her house. The other goes to a place I haven't told her about yet.

"You want to see something?" I ask.

Brianna smiles in the passenger seat. "That's an awful pickup line."

Her retort is rewarded with a bark of a laugh. A real laugh. My hand twists on the leather steering wheel of my truck and I let that warmth flow through me. It's an unfamiliar feeling to me now. I used to laugh like this all the time. Not in the last two years. Not while she was gone.

"I'm for real, though," I tell her as we slow at the first stop sign. Main Street is lit with lampposts and the streets are quiet on this side of town.

"Is this one of your ulterior motives?" she asks, turning her head, but still remaining leaned back in the seat. She's so fucking gorgeous, relaxed and happy. I fucking missed her. I missed her more than anything.

"I got a house by the lake," I admit to her after clearing my throat.

"What?" That gets her attention and she sits a little straighter, her emerald eyes a little wider.

"By Crystal Lake. I bought the property a while back and had a house built. The structure's all done."

"Really?" Her voice is soft. Filled with awe and maybe nostalgia for the way we used to be. "We used to say we would."

"I know." A smile comes to my face, and I don't force it away.

There's a beat and then another in my chest. Just friends, I remind myself ... but maybe friends with benefits.

The night's cool and fresh. The darkness outside

the car seems to make the world smaller. It's just me and her. Nobody watching. Bri is gorgeous in the light from the console. She looks like I pictured she would, back in high school. "You want to see it?"

Without hesitation she answers, "Yes. I really do." She bites down on her lower lip to keep from grinning any wider.

All I can do is nod for a moment, happy she wants to see it.

"It's still being built and all," I say in warning, suddenly feeling a little self-conscious about it. "The interior's not done. I put in the electric last week."

"Are you doing it yourself?"

"Yeah," I say and now that nervousness is replaced by pride.

"Some of the guys are helping here and there. Small-town handyman, small-town mechanic."

"As if you only fix cars," Bri teases.

I almost say I fix broken hearts too, but I stop myself. It's cheesy and it's pushing it. I definitely haven't fixed her broken heart. I'm the one who broke it in the first place and I may not be the smartest, but I know my limits.

So I don't push it and an easy quiet falls between us as she turns up a song she says she loves. It's a new one for me. I haven't heard it but watching what it does to her, hell, I love it now too.

We get to the fork in the road and I take the one that leads down to Crystal Lake.

"Was this your plan all along?" she questions and I shake my head.

"No, I just wanted to take you home, I swear."

She looks me up and down with her lips pursed.

"Scout's honor," I tell her, raising my hand and giving her a nod.

"It just hit me when we got in the truck. I promise."

Having a house on the lake is one of the dreams we had together. One we talked about as early as high school, before we had any business talking about buying houses or owning property together. I didn't have a dollar to my name but I said I'd buy her whatever house she wanted on the lake.

The thought of it was exciting for us both. A little house. Privacy. A door to shut everybody else out with. No one would be able to walk in on us.

That's what I built. Our getaway.

My heart races and I didn't expect that at all.

It's just a house. If anyone asks, I built the house for me, but of course Brianna's been in the back of my mind all this time. How could she not be? How could

I not think of her when I was building our dream place on the lake?

"Have you been thinking about getting a place now that you're back?" I ask and attempt to sound casual. The thoughts in my head are shitty company compared to her voice.

She glances out the window, thoughtful. "I'm staying with my parents for a while. Right now, I'm still planning on working two jobs for the foreseeable."

"Are you sure you want to do that?" I question as I turn down the gravel road. "You won't get burned out?"

"I just want to pay off my student loans as fast as I can, you know?"

Brianna's eyes meet mine again and I'll be damned if it isn't just how it was before. I keep thinking it and I know it's not right, but it can't be denied. The way she talks to me, all her hopes and dreams coming up to the surface, it's like it was. It gives me hope.

I force it away. If this is all I can have, if Bri telling me what she really wants from her life is all I can have as her friend, I'll sure as hell take it.

"I get that," I answer, keeping it somewhat surface

level. "I tried to pay off my car as soon as I could too. I don't want debt hanging over my head."

"Me neither," she agrees. "It makes me nervous. Not because I don't think I'll be able to pay, just because …"

"Because it's hanging over your head. Bothering you all the time."

"Exactly." She bites at her lip. "You never know when something might happen. I like to have everything tidied up just in case, and I want the same thing for my loans. Plus it'll be easier to move on once those are paid off."

"Move on to what?" An anxiousness spikes through me.

"I don't know. I was for real when I said that to your mom. My biggest plan is to pay off the loans. They're not too expensive, and then I'll get a little savings together. Maybe then I'll make more permanent decisions." Bri laughs again. It's the prettiest sound I've ever heard. "Or maybe I won't. Who knows?"

"Not moving away though, right?" I ask her and dammit, I sound like a downright fool.

"No, Asher. I don't think I'm moving and if I do, it won't be far."

Swallowing hard, I nod and then nod again.

"I just want to be debt-free if I can be."

"Smart. You always have been." I agree with her decision. I like that she's safe living with her parents too. I like that she's not living alone.

I'd like it more if she lived with me, though. I bite my tongue to keep those words from coming out. I already got down on my knees once today. I'm not going farther.

Friendship, I remind myself again. This is about friendship.

A friend would show her his place. A friend wouldn't put any pressure on the moment. A friend would just share it with her. No expectations.

The gravel crunches under the wheels as we pull in. Crystal Lake is a decent size. Not too big, not too small. Waves lap at the sandy shore. It's calm out here, and quiet, with more stars than you can see in town. It's a small enough town that there's plenty of night sky even when you're standing on Main Street, but out here they're even brighter and clearer.

There's a row of houses, each one slightly different yet they all have that beachy feel to them. Mine is at the end of the row, set back a little bit from the others. It had a bigger yard. That's why I got it; I liked the lot. More space for the house and more privacy.

We pull up and climb out of the truck, and I sink into my memories again as the doors close with a gentle thud in the night.

We went out on the lake so many times growing up. The girls would sunbathe. Sometimes we'd go fishing—all of us guys, girls, it didn't matter. What mattered was that everybody was happy. My friends laughed. That's what summer meant. The sound of Brianna's laughter, a splash as somebody did a cannonball, whoever got splashed would holler, and we would all just let go.

With nostalgia clinging to me, I turn to my right in front of what will be my home to see Brianna staring up at it like she can't believe it's here. "This is your place?"

"This is it."

She glances at me, and I'm not sure what to make of her expression. It's so hopeful. It's so familiar.

It scares the shit out of me.

Brianna steps a little closer to the house, looks a little harder.

Anxiety races through me with every fraction of a second that goes by. My heart sinks. This isn't what she pictured, then. This isn't what she wanted. The dream we had together always felt clear to me. I'd be fooling myself if I said I didn't build this house off the specifics of that dream.

Maybe I had it wrong. Maybe I had everything wrong.

"It's not even halfway done," I find myself saying. "There's a little bit left to do on the exterior, and the interior's a mess. I may take parts of it out and start over. I don't know if—"

She cuts me off and tells me, "Asher, this place is amazing. It's absolutely perfect."

All I can think, and thank fuck I don't say it, is *I built it for you.*

Chapter 11

Brianna

ASHER'S HOUSE IS LIKE SOMETHING OUT OF our dreams. I can't help thinking it. I can't help feeling like I belong in this place.

I haven't put a penny into it. I didn't even know it existed and yet I'm touching every little piece of drywall and every finish.

I have no right and I damn well know it, but I love this place already.

This is pretty close to what I pictured back in school, when we would write notes to each other and joke about the house we were going to build on the lake. It doesn't escape me that there's a wraparound porch. The question is right there on the tip of my tongue whether or not he remembered that I wanted one.

"There's still a lot to do," Asher says while walking

me through room by room and he isn't lying. It's not even close to being finished, at least not from what I see. But I can see how it'll be when it's done.

We all loved the lake. That was where we spent our summers. Out on rafts or in fishing boats, lying on the beach, screwing around the way kids screw around. I know why we loved it. It's because the summer was always carefree. Everybody was always happy. The days were long, and there was enough time to do everything we wanted to do.

Memories hit me hard.

Of course, back then, I didn't understand that we were the freest we might ever be in our lives. We had no bills to pay and no jobs to go to except when we worked our shifts at the ice cream shop or one of the stores downtown. The stakes weren't very high.

My heart hadn't been broken yet.

As we walk through the house, I find myself standing closer to him, looking at him more than the house. What the hell is wrong with me? I'm still the same lovesick girl I've always been for him. No matter how much I wish I wasn't.

"They're going in soon, but we need to fix a few things first," Asher states and then looks back at me.

Tucking my hair behind my ear I take a good hard

look around the kitchen as if it's what should be occupying my mind right now.

The cabinets are lined up in the kitchen, but there's no countertops. This is a place in the process of becoming what it will be. This is the beginning of reality.

"The whole place smells like sawdust," I comment just to say something and Asher laughs. I missed that sound.

There are little piles of it in all the corners. It makes my heart beat hard in my throat. We would've done this together if we'd followed our dreams.

I push away the feeling of sadness because of the look on his face. He's obviously proud. A little smile curves the corners of his lips. He keeps glancing at me like a puppy dog wanting my approval.

I'm more than eager to give it.

When we first started dating, my sister called him a lovesick puppy dog because he followed me everywhere. He just wanted to spend time with me.

"I'm proud of you, Ash," I say like a friend would. "We should celebrate. This is incredible." And I find myself thinking of *ulterior motives*.

"Hmm." He pretends to consider this seriously. "Celebrations are usually reserved for when you finish the house."

"No," I tell him. "This is just as good. This is taking a

real step. It's saying what you want in life and then going for it. It's amazing. You don't happen to have champagne in those cupboards, do you?"

His smile falters, but he puts it right back into place with a laugh. "No. I wouldn't trust this water yet, either." He chuckles and I let out a gentle laugh too.

The space between us heats.

I just have to be closer to him. I'm alone with him. This is what we always wanted.

A place we could go to get away from everyone else. A place we could be without our parents knocking on the door. A place where there were no rules or curfew. A real place of our own.

"Is it hot in here?" I ask and I reach for my shirt before I realize what I'm doing and start to unbutton it.

Asher's eyes darken. His breathing picks up.

I get the top button undone, then the next. He watches with hungry eyes as my fingers work over them.

He swallows hard. Keeps his hands firmly in his pockets. His eyes trail back up my skin to my face.

"Brianna," he warns in a tone I fucking love. A tone I haven't heard in far too long. It's the darker side of the tone he used in the bar when he told me not to be bad. This time he means it. This time he means he won't be able to hold back.

"What?" I say as if I have no idea what I'm doing,

slipping the shirt off my shoulders. I have a cami on underneath, and a lace bra peeks through. There's still more to go. He could still stop me if he wanted. The bulge in his pants says he doesn't want to stop me.

"I thought we were friends," he says.

"Who said we weren't friends?" I counter.

"You said you wanted to be friends first." His voice is thick with how much he wants this. I recognize that voice on him.

Asher can't pretend that he doesn't want me. He can't pretend that he's only thinking of platonic friendship.

"Aren't you the one who suggested friends with benefits?" I ask him. "Or were you just teasing me?" I arch an eyebrow.

He only smirks and lets his gaze drift down my body. Never once have I felt self-conscious in front of him. Even now, he groans in need. Like I'm testing him.

As if I'm the one who's been doing that. He's been pushing me all night.

The image of his body on mine lights every nerve ending in me on fire. I think of that back room at the bar. Every hot illicit thought I've had about him, filters in one by one. Not just the ones since we broke up, but always. I wanted him this way before I was even fully aware of what wanting him meant as a woman. That's how long I've loved Asher.

I pull my cami over my head. He stops and stares as if he hasn't seen me naked before. As if this is truly the most beautiful sight he's ever seen. I could be standing in front of the Wonders of the World, and he'd still only see me.

He shakes his head a bit, his thumb resting on his bottom lip.

"Friends," he says again, and I know what he's doing. He's trying to give me what I wanted and put a stop to this. I demanded that we start with friendship. I begged him for it.

I wanted to slow down, but tonight?

Tonight I need it to speed up.

The dream is moving on without me, and I won't miss it. At least, I won't miss it tonight.

This might be the only chance Asher and I have to be together in the house we dreamed of in high school. This might be the only chance we have to live out those fantasies.

I'm done not taking chances. I'm done second-guessing my actions.

I stop thinking and act. I'll worry about tomorrow when it comes and not a moment before.

I reach for my bra, but Asher takes a step forward,

stopping me. He strides closer and closer until I have to look up to look into his face. His hand comes down over mine.

"Are you sure about this?" he asks. "Are you absolutely sure? Because it was supposed to be about friendship, Bri. That's what it was supposed to be about."

His hand holds my wrist ever so gently, and I know it's because he wants to be the one to take my bra off if we're going to do this. And if we're not, he wants to be the one to help me put my clothes back on.

"There is such a thing as friends with benefits," I say.

His eyes flare with surprise. "Friends with benefits," he repeats. "You fucking with me, Bri baby?"

I shake my head once. "Nope."

"What kind of friends, with exactly what benefits?" he questions, releasing me and pacing around me so I have to turn around.

"Like the sexual kind. The fun kind." Sex has always been fun for us. Fun and sensual. We've always matched each other that way. Always had a good time. It was a release from the world, and God knows we both need that.

"If you give that to me, I won't be able to stop. I want you too much."

"I like your honesty," I tell him. "I've always liked that about you."

"So … do you want to give it a try?" His voice is pure heat.

"Being friends with benefits?"

"Yes," he says, "and just to be clear, that means that I would fuck you in this house tonight, Brianna. That's what it would mean. I just want to make sure we understand each other."

"We've always understood each other." I step forward, moving his hand onto the clasp of my bra.

Asher pauses, but it's not hesitation. He's using the moment to memorize me. He knows this could be our only shot. He knows nothing is promised to us in life. He knows we haven't agreed on a future yet.

He knows.

His fingers twist. The clasp of my bra unhooks, and he lets it fall to the unfinished floor.

Chapter 12

Asher

THE BRA FALLS TO THE FLOOR WITH A SOFT rustle and all I can hear is her heavy breathing. Her chest rises and falls with every deep inhale. Every move I make is deliberate, from my fingers spearing through her hair and bringing her forward so I can take her lips with mine, to how the tip of my tongue slips along her seam until she moans and grants me entry. I lay my jacket down while she catches her breath, so she can lay on it. I've barely got it in place, before she kisses me again. Deepening the kiss, I pull her body toward mine. One hand is still in her hair with the other on her hip. My thumb slips along the waistline of her pants and when she pulls back ever so slightly to breathe, inviting a touch of cooler air in the heated space between us, I work the button in the front and then slip her jeans down her legs.

I don't hesitate. With her pussy practically bared to me and only a thin piece of fabric separating us, I lean forward and suck right where I know her clit is. I'm not gentle in the least, nipping at the lace fabric. Her gasp is joined by both of her hands flying to my shoulders. The jeans are still tangled around her ankles and she can hardly move.

Gripping her thighs to hold her still, I do it again.

"Asher." She moans my name and I fucking love it.

In a quick move, I grab her ass and pull her down to the subfloor with me. The shriek she gives has a hint of humor that comes with the feminine laugh that makes me smile. She'll be crying out my name soon, though.

With both hands I pull her panties down, leaving her bared to me. Tossing them and her jeans into the puddle of clothes beside us, I get on my knees and stare down at Bri. Naked and peering up at me with lust and desire, with confidence and wanting.

I fucking love you, Bri.

How many times have I said it? Not enough.

The confession stays silent as I spread her legs wide enough for my shoulders and give her slit a languid lick. Fuck. I groan into her heat and her thighs clench around me as her back arches. I suck and massage my tongue against her clit. She bucks her hips and I don't bother to hold her down. I love what I do to her.

"Already wet for me, Bri baby?" I murmur and she stares up at me with flushed cheeks.

"I'm close already." Her admission is breathless.

Bracing myself with one hand and towering over her, I push two fingers inside of her and curve them, stroking that sweet spot of hers.

"I know just how to get you off," I tell her as her head falls back and her neck arches. The unfinished kitchen is expansive and filled with her moans as I bring her closer to the edge.

Just as her toes curl and her bottom lip drops, I pull out of her, bringing my fingers to my lips.

"Mmm." I lick her arousal from my fingers and when I glance back down, a wide-eyed Bri is desperately waiting. She writhes in need but I wait a moment longer.

"You know how many times I've gotten you off with my tongue?" I question her and then lean down, licking, sucking and nipping her.

Her answer is incoherent as her nails scrape along my scalp and she rocks herself into my tongue. Her heel comes up on my shoulder as she squirms on the floor, eager and desperate.

Goddamn she tastes so sweet. I would devour her

without a second thought, but I'm not ready to let her get off just yet.

Just as her moans get louder, just as she reaches the edge again, I pull back. Her hands slip and she stares up at me, irritation flashing in those gorgeous green eyes.

"I'm close, Asher, please," she barely gets out and those hands of hers turn to fists, coming down to hit the ground.

I can't help but chuckle.

"And I'm rock hard for you. Pretty sure there's pre-cum leaking just for you."

She reaches up, her expression turning sultry again as she bites her bottom lip. "Then fuck me, come inside me," she whispers, her hands wrapping around my back to bring me down to lie on top of her.

If I were a weaker man, I'd lose myself in this moment. It's everything I've ever wanted with her. My shirt comes off first and then I kick my jeans off. All the while her hands roam my body. All the while she whispers that she needs me. All the while my heart hammers, needing her just the same.

I lower myself, leaving openmouthed kisses along her neck as I thrust inside her to the hilt.

"Asher!" she screams at the same time that I groan in unadulterated pleasure. A cold sweat breaks out along my skin. I can't move just yet, she's so fucking tight. I give her a moment to adjust and as I do, I repeat what she's said, "Friends with benefits?" I pull out slowly, then slam back in.

"Yes," she tells me as her head thrashes from one side and then the other.

I pull back out, slowly again and sit up enough to move my thumb to her clit. Her walls flutter around my cock instantly. "You're so close."

All she can do is breathe and nod in agreement.

It's then that I kiss her, deeply, but I stop moving altogether and she breaks the kiss, begging me, "Please, Asher."

"Tell me we're more than friends," I command, still very much deep inside of her.

Wide eyed and with her mouth still parted, she stares up in shock. Almost as if she didn't hear me.

"Tell me that we are more than just friends with benefits. That there's something else here between us, something that friends don't have."

Nerves prick at the back of my neck and she's silent.

I rock inside of her once and then again. Her expression softens and her head lolls back. "Asher," she moans and I kiss her neck.

I'm harder, deeper, bringing her to the edge again and the moment she's close, I stop.

Her fists hit the floor beneath us in frustration.

"Please, Asher!"

"Tell me the truth. Say it, Bri. And I'll fuck you so hard you'll feel it all week. You'll know exactly who you belong to."

Something gives way inside of her, and open vulnerability shines in her eyes. "We are more than friends."

I half expect her to push me away, judging from the look in her eyes. Instead she leans up and kisses me, in a desperate way. In a way that it's obvious she needs me.

When I break the kiss, her eyes are glossy.

"Bri baby, I need to hear that you feel this too."

"I don't—" she starts and instead of finishing her thought, she merely grabs my forearms as if I would get up and walk away if she wasn't holding me where I am. As if that could ever be a possibility.

"I don't want to be friends with benefits … I want to fuck you because you're mine." She's silent beneath me, on the verge of breaking, I can feel it.

She almost speaks; her lips move but nothing comes. "Tell me you're mine, Bri."

"You're going to break my heart again," she admits to me, her voice cracking. I'm quick to kiss her, to rock myself against her and her body reacts instantly. Primed and ready for nothing but the pleasure I'm going to give her.

I breathe out against the shell of her ear and tell

her, "I'm not a smart man, Bri, but I'm not that fucking stupid." I thrust in and out again and again.

"Tell me you're mine," I command and she whispers in the crook of my neck, "I'm yours."

"That's what I needed, Bri baby," I murmur along her skin and pepper kisses on every inch of her before picking up my pace and fucking her just like I promised I would. It doesn't take long for her to come all over my dick. The moment she comes, I pull her knees up, angling her just right, and piston my hips to fuck her harder and deeper.

She gets off three times before I finally reach my own orgasm and we both lie naked beside each other catching our breath.

Even fully clothed again, it's a touch cold in the empty house. The nights will do that and the breeze from the open windows adds to the chill.

I fucking love it, though, because it means she's molded her body to mine. She hasn't let go of me other than to let me clean her up and for us to get dressed.

"You never did things like that before." Her whisper breaks the silence.

"Things like what?"

"Like bringing my knees up ... and like not letting me ... get off," she comments and then buries her head into my shoulder, like she's embarrassed.

A hum leaves me, one of satisfaction. "I think you'll remember tonight, won't you?" My tone is slightly arrogant and it makes her laugh. The cocky side of me always did amuse her.

She clears her throat after readjusting and her fingers play along my chest.

"I just ... I want to know ..." The hesitation isn't like her and I don't know what she's tiptoeing around. A crease settles in my forehead and it's not until she starts her question that it hits me what she's getting at, "Did you do that with other—"

"No." I'm quick to cut her off. "Stop those thoughts right now, Bri. It's only ever been you."

She stills at my side before looking up at me, her gaze and expression serious. "You've only ever been with me?"

I nod, letting her know it's true. As if there was anyone else in this small town I'd ever want. Everything about this place is a reminder of her, including the people in it.

Her expression turns remorseful. It's in the way her lips part and the way her eyes shine. It's not like I didn't see she was with other guys. I have social media just like she does. I know she went out. I don't give a shit. I don't care what happened before.

"You are my only, Bri. And I don't care if or who or what happened while you were away."

I thought my statement would soothe whatever she's feeling, but there's some kind of residual guilt in her eyes as she fidgets with her necklace. Turning over to my side so I'm facing her, I lean down and kiss her forehead and then run the tip of my nose along hers.

"Nothing matters except the two of us right now."

She nods and then peeks back up at me. I know that look. I'll be damned if tonight is ruined with her overthinking, with her wishing things we can't change now were different.

I let out a small groan and kiss her neck before whispering, "Bri baby, I need you again. Strip down for me. Let me love on you."

A spark of heat ignites instantly and my Bri kisses me at the same time that she unbuttons her pants. Eager and wanting. Mine. And that's all that fucking matters.

Chapter 13

Brianna

EVEN THOUGH I'M AT WORK, I CAN'T FOCUS. I
don't think anybody would be surprised to hear
it. Readjusting in my seat reminds me of the
ache between my legs and I close my eyes to keep from
making that situation audible.

My main goal today is keeping my cool so that my
mother or sister, or anyone else in this office building,
doesn't notice anything is out of the ordinary. The problem is that I can't get my mind off Asher and because
of that, I can't seem to do a darn thing right.

Even as simple as printing out a listing. It took me
three tries to print out the correct address fifteen minutes ago. Autumn has been occasionally staring ever
since.

She has to know something's up, but I have no

intention of telling a soul. Not until I even know what to say. My gaze lifts to the large clock on the front wall. I'm waiting for both the big and little hands to hit 12:00 so I can leave for lunch.

My mind has been spinning in circles since last night. Every thought is full of him. And the office isn't giving me any distractions. My project today, other than messing up simple side tasks, is looking up comps for Asher's family home.

Freaking great.

Every other thought that crosses my mind is his name. Or his deep tone whispering my name. Or his warm breath on the side of my neck, giving me shivers. Or the tortured groans of pleasure he made all last night. He told me everything I've wanted to hear for two years. Asher said everything I could've dreamed. I've missed him more than anything, and it felt so right to be together.

My phone pings and I'm quick to reach it for no other reason than to be distracted. It's not Asher, and the amount of disappointment I feel is ridiculous. He's working. I'm working. I click over to my texts and read the "good morning, beautiful" message he sent me. Instantly, my lips lift up into a smirk.

But it's not him who messaged me now.

Katelyn: *What are you up to, Bri?*

Brianna: *Missing you!*

My smirk turns to a full-blown smile. I haven't heard from Katelyn in like a week. In other words, since all of this went down ... since Asher went down. The smirk returns.

Katelyn: *It's been too long and I was thinking of you!*

I'm quick to text her back. If Renee is my rock here, Katelyn was my rock at university. The memories give me those warm fuzzy feelings and my fingers fly across my phone as we chat.

Each of us went back home after college. Katelyn understands what it's like. You're different when you go back. How could you not be? Four years passed while I was away. Sometimes I went through hell and heartbreak. It makes you see the world in an entirely new way. I still have warm, nostalgic feelings about home, but I see it differently now. I can't help it. I even see Asher with new eyes.

Are they really that new, though? I still miss him. I still want him.

Katelyn: *Tell me what's going on? I haven't heard a peep from you since you started your job ... and you didn't tell me what happened when Asher picked up your car.*

Chewing on the inside of my cheek, I debate on what and how to tell her. Katelyn was with me when I got the call from Asher. He started out by saying he couldn't come up to see me at college, and I …

I just lost it. The memory hits me hard and I know it hit her hard too. 'Cause like I said, she was my rock.

"You were supposed to come last weekend," I said, my voice shaking. "You didn't, and now you're not coming again. You don't care about seeing me. It's not a priority for you."

"Of course you're a priority, Bri. I obviously care about you," he answered.

"It's not obvious," I shot back. "You don't call me unless it's to cancel. You don't respond to texts for hours. Sometimes days." I was crying by then. Tears streaming down my face. Katelyn came and stood by my side. "I don't want to break up with you. I just want you to be here. It feels like it's over between us."

I wanted to say more. I wanted him to understand me, and be close to me the way he always had.

But as I took a breath, he cut me off.

"Fine." Asher's voice sounded angry and tired and thin. "It's over."

Then he hung up, leaving me standing there, the phone trembling in my hand. I'd never cried so hard in my life. Katelyn wrapped her arms around me, waiting until I caught my breath. When she asked me who broke up with who, I didn't have an answer.

I still don't have an answer.

Which was it? Asher not coming to see me, or me pushing him too hard? I don't know.

Faced with the idea of telling Katelyn what happened and just shutting up and telling her I'm at work, I choose the latter. I'm not ready to make this real. I'm not ready to rehash everything all over again. It seems like ... Asher wants us to have it together. He's been holding on to this dream just like I have.

But ... are we together? Is it even possible?

A tap, tap, tap at the edge of my desk nearly has me throwing my phone and jumping out of my seat. It's my mother, with a cocked brow looking down at me from her thin gold-rimmed glasses and burgundy cardigan.

"Sorry," I push out and lay my phone face down on the desk. My cheeks flush with embarrassment. I'm a better employee than this.

"Are you okay, hon?" I look up at her and see wide eyes of concern. Concern from a mother, not a boss. And I consider lying. Or brushing it off. But she gives me a sympathetic smile with her voice low and gentle. "I heard about you and Asher."

And then my chin trembles like I'm going to cry. Well, I'm not. Not here at the office. I press my lips together, grab a tissue, and dab at the corners of my eyes. Oddly enough my desk is the only desk with a tissue box on it.

I try to avoid my mother's gaze, only to find my sister's. The same sympathetic look is in her expression.

It's like being cornered, and the truth slips out before I know what I'm doing.

"I'm afraid," I admit, balling up the tissue, and then check to make sure nobody else will overhear. It would be fine if Autumn did, but there are three other people here and they don't need to know. It's not their business and if they knew, it would be the whole town's business. "I'm afraid that if I give my heart to him again, he's going to break it."

Shoot. Now it doesn't matter that I'm in the office. It doesn't matter that I'm at work, or even that my mom is standing here. Hot tears slip down my face, trickling from the outer corners before I can control it. I'm embarrassed by the tears, but at least I'm not alone. My mom rubs my back. It's silent at least. And over quickly. I don't even know how or why, but I'm a complete mess today.

Because I know I am not a match for Asher Hart and he's probably going to break my heart again.

I'm not even aware Autumn's beside me until her hand is on my shoulder.

"Oh my God, Bri, what's going on?" She joins my mom in hovering over me, worried. "Is this the Asher thing?" She keeps her voice hushed but still, I'm sure the office is going to figure out there's something going on. To hell with it. I don't care if they think I've lost it. It is what it is.

Pulling more tissues out with a vengeance, I answer my sister, "Yes. I'm scared to get back together with him. If I give him my heart and he breaks it all over again, I don't know what I'll do."

Autumn laughs, her voice low. "I don't think you ever took your heart back. So you might as well give it a shot."

"What?" I stare up at her and she gives me a sad smile even though her eyes are hopeful. "You never took your heart back, Bri."

She has a point. Even though we broke up, part of me always belonged to Asher. I couldn't keep him out of my dreams or the random thoughts I'd have throughout the day. Everywhere I went, there he was.

So I thought there was really no point in avoiding home, when it was the only place I wanted to be. There was no point in making things harder for myself by not taking the job at my mom's office, when he would be here too. The only way I wouldn't have come home, would have been if he'd moved on.

"Can I forgive and forget? Do I even need to forgive him and forget? Can't we just move on together?" I don't know why I list the questions and all my mom does is say, "Oh, sweetie."

It's quiet a moment while the two of them share a look.

"Have you talked to Renee?" Autumn asks.

I shake my head. She messaged to check on me but I asked her for space.

"'Cause you didn't want to tell her?" she guesses and I only nod. She gets it. I'm grateful my family gets it. Renee understands too. "She'll be there if you need her," Autumn says and I already know that. Just like I'm there for her ... if ever she had something to say about Griffin.

"He's a good guy, Brianna. I've always thought that."

"He broke up with me."

Mom arches an eyebrow. "It sounded pretty mutual, from what you said."

"We were both unhappy." I take a deep breath and toss the used tissues, vowing that I'm done with crying. "But he was the one who ended it."

"Please," Autumn says. "He is a cinnamon roll puppy

dog who might as well follow you around panting. That's just who he is. He's always been like that and he always will be."

My mom laughs and I can't help the little bubble of laughter that escapes from me even though it sounds pathetic.

"Honestly, Bri?" Autumn puts a no-nonsense expression on her face. "He would pee circles around you if he could."

"Okay." My mom raises a hand. She admonishes my sister, "That's very crude, Autumn."

The two of us laugh, though, very much in spite of myself.

Autumn shrugs. "You okay, Bri?"

"I'll be fine."

I take big, deep breaths and calm down. I'm done now. I've cried. I've felt my feelings. Now it's time to focus on work like the grown woman I am.

"I didn't mean to interrupt your conversation," my mother says and then she tells Autumn to get back to it. With a pat on the back, she leaves me be but tells me I can head home early if I need.

I need to buy them both flowers the next time I'm out. Or chocolate or something nice.

Pulling my hair back into a makeshift ponytail, I pull myself together, one breath at a time.

I've already had a full crying session and it's not even lunch. Ugh.

My phone lights up and I assume it's a message from Katelyn as I let my hair fall and reach for it. There's a hard beat in my chest when I see it's a message from Asher.

I force myself to pick up my phone casually, as if getting a text from him is no big deal.

Asher: *We didn't get to have breakfast together. Want me to bring you lunch at work?*

Chewing on my bottom lip, I glance at my mom and then my sister, both of whom are back to work tapping at their keyboards … like I should be.

I text him back: *I want to have lunch with you, but you don't have to drop it off.*

Asher: *I don't?*

Brianna: *I can step away for a few minutes. I want to talk to you.*

Asher: *Okay.*

His next message takes a little more time.

Asher: *If you want to get away, let's do that.*

Asher: *Meet me at the bakery?*

Chapter 14

Asher

"I WANT TO TALK."

Fucking hell. Why, woman? That's all I wanted to text her. Bri's always overthinking, always worried about what's happening the day after next.

Everything is good, better than good. We're the way we were meant to be. It's easy. But I know exactly what those words mean. It's not like it's the first time she's told me: I want to talk.

Hell, the last time she said that, I wanted to talk too. I wanted to tell her my father got drunk and when Mom tried to take the bottle away, he hit her. I wanted to tell her he's not okay and I'm not okay either. He's a better man than that, but he's an alcoholic and we don't know what to do.

I remember it all, balled up at the back of my throat. When I found out the bills weren't paid. When everything came down on my shoulders and I was fucking drowning. All I wanted was to tell her everything.

But my mother didn't. She didn't want anyone to know.

I had to protect them all. I had to step up and be a man.

I had to protect everyone involved. I didn't want to betray my dad by telling anyone outside our family what he'd done. That's not the kind of man he is. And I didn't want Bri to risk coming home to try and fix things for herself. Not when she was living her dream.

I couldn't be a burden to her.

Bri was off at college, and she didn't need to come back for me.

My stomach knots as I walk down Main Street. My palms sweat. Why does she want to talk so much? I love the sound of her voice, but we could just … not talk. I just want us to be. Bri overthinks everything, and she doesn't have to. We click. We work. I felt it last night.

It should be that simple.

An older lady I've worked for before, Martina, comes out of the antique store she owns just as I'm going by. "Oh, Asher, I'm glad to see you. Do you have a second?"

"'Of course I do." Glancing down the street to Melissa's Sweets, I know Bri will see me from here if she's there. Slipping my hands in my pockets, I ask Mrs. Brown what she needs. Her husband passed a few years ago and she took over the business. We thought she might retire, but she said she loves the shop too much. A picture of the two of them, posed in front of the two-story building with bright blue shutters, hangs in the front room. It's from the day they opened and I just repainted those blue shutters for her last year I think it was.

Martina gestures up at the sign hanging above the door. It's got a crack in it, and the blue on it has faded. "Must have been the wind," she comments and then turns to face me. "Do you think you can fix it for me?"

With Brody and Griffin's new bar and its shiny front open for business, every other place is updating their exterior. All of Main Street is sprucing up. Which means I'm getting calls left and right. And stopped outside of shops too.

I crane my neck side to side, looking at the crack in the old sign. "I think I can. Shouldn't take me too long so long as it's just the sign." I look back to Martina. She's got wrinkles around her eyes but the same smile I remember from my childhood. "I can make you a new one if you'd like."

Her whole face lights up. Martina clasps her hands in front of her chest. "That would be wonderful, Asher. Thank you."

"I'll call you, promise," I tell her, giving a short wave and a smile. I make a mental note to follow through.

"I'll be waiting," she says. "No rush, though, really. When you've got the time."

I smile and nod and keep moving toward the bakery. Then my blood runs cold and my entire body is paralyzed.

No.

A familiar car is parked on the opposite side of the street.

No.

Not Brianna's car. My dad's.

It can't be his car outside of the liquor store.

No.

My feet move of their own accord, across from the bakery and out to his car. As I get closer, I spot his air freshener hanging from the rearview mirror and a piece of mail he's had on the dashboard for three months. Nervousness pricks down my back.

I don't even want to look, but I can't help it. Barely breathing, I spot him right there, in broad daylight, putting a six-pack on the counter.

No.

I'm barely aware of following him. I just do it. I check for traffic and cross in the middle of the block. The bell on the door chimes as I open it and get hit with a cool blast of air-conditioning and the smell of floor polish.

My dad's still at the counter. It's a normal scene for everybody but him. The clerk, Miss Jean, is happy as can be and smiling at my dad. She has no idea what happened at our house.

His eyes flick up toward the door. Toward me. He does a double take.

Betrayal seeps through me, flooding every other emotion.

And then his face flushes a deep red. He fumbles in his pocket for his wallet and takes out cash.

"What's that for?" I ask, my voice too loud. There's so much rage pounding through me that my voice shakes.

The clerk smiles at me, although it falters. She knows who I am. Everybody around here does. She just doesn't know about my dad's problem.

"Just his weekly pickup," the clerk answers.

Weekly? I can barely stand upright. No.

"What?" I'm going to lose my shit. My vision goes dark at the edges. "Weekly?"

My father's voice is stern when he says, "I think you should step outside, Son."

Miss Jean doesn't respond to me. She glances between the two of us before taking the money from his hand silently and nervously pops the drawer on the register.

I can't believe he's buying beer.

"Do you dump it down the drain?" I question sarcastically and then immediately shake my head. "Of course you don't." Spite coats my conclusion before he even has a chance to respond.

Taking one step forward Miss Jean asks, "You okay, Asher?"

My father tries to answer her, motioning in the air, but my next step gets his attention before he can say a damn thing.

"Are you drinking?"

My father just looks at me, his face hard and ashamed. He licks his lips and his gaze drops to the floor before coming back up. He's silent. He's not going to answer. I caught him red-handed, and he won't answer.

The clerk looks between the two of us, obviously uncomfortable.

"How long?" I keep my voice even and low, but she doesn't answer. Probably because I'm still looking at my father. I have to force myself to face Miss Jean. "How long has he been picking up weekly beer?" I do my damnedest to be polite, to keep my tone as friendly as I can. But I don't know how successful I am.

My hands are shaking so fucking bad, I struggle to ball them into fists. I'm far too aware I'm hardly contained.

I keep myself in check, barely, because I'm a good guy, a good person, and I won't do what I want to do. Because what I want is to knock down all the alcohol in this place. Smash every bottle on the floor until no one else can drink it. Miss Jean doesn't deserve that. No one does. Not when all of this rage is only for my father.

"You lied. How could you do this to us?" My voice cracks and it only makes me clench my fists tighter.

"Asher," my dad warns.

"Is everything okay?" Miss Jean reaches toward the phone on her counter, probably wanting to call someone for help, finally putting the pieces together.

"Everything's fine." My dad gives her a smile. "It's fine."

Judging from the sadness and regret in her gaze, she doesn't believe my father. Thank God for that, because it's not fine. Nothing is okay right now.

"You're an alcoholic who doesn't work. Where are you even getting the money for this?"

My dad puts his hands around the bag on the counter. "We can talk about this later."

My control slips, my voice getting louder by the second.

"I took over the bills. I took over everything." I practically yell and I wish I could stop. "Every damn thing at home. I tried to make it okay." I can't shut up. I know better than to do this. I know better than to tell the whole town our business. Airing out our dirty laundry and embarrassing my mother.

I just tried so hard.

"You don't have any bills." My voice cracks on a shout. The stress of the last two years comes over me like a block of concrete. Like a broken sign snapping off a pole. This isn't fixable. What he's doing isn't fixable. "All you had to do was take care of Ma. That's all you had to do. And really? All you had to do was take care of yourself. She was fine. She's good. She wanted you to get better."

I have to stop, but I can't.

"This was supposed to be your retirement!" My voice echoes in the store. I hope to God nobody else is in here. I can't keep these feelings bottled up for one more second. "All you had to do was stop fucking drinking."

As I heave in a breath, trying to steady myself,

trying to stop from falling into that dark place again, Miss Jean tells me it's okay. She says, "It's okay, son. It's going to be okay." But she doesn't know the half of it and I'm not her son.

I can barely look up at her to tell her, "It's not okay. He's an alcoholic and an angry drunk."

Miss Jean freezes, her face going white. She has no idea what to do. Neither do I. What's a person supposed to do in this situation? My dad's an alcoholic, but he's a grown man. It's not illegal for him to walk into a liquor store and buy whatever he wants.

I want to drag him out of here, shove him into his car, and take him home so I can repeat all this until he gets it through his head. But some part of me knows that it won't. It can't. If he hasn't figured this out by now, he's not going to. I don't know how else to explain it to him.

In all of this, watching me break down, my father reaches up for the six-pack.

All I can see is red as he does it. What was the point of covering for him? What was the point of breaking up with Bri? I gave her up because I thought there would be light at the end of the tunnel. I thought my dad would end up okay. I thought I might have another chance at the life I had to put on pause.

"What are you doing?" I question him as the bottles

clink together in the cardboard carrier. "You don't give a shit, do you?"

What the hell do I do? Cut him off? Never speak to him again? I don't know. I don't even know how I'm supposed to leave the situation at the store. All I know is that I'm not okay.

"Son," my dad says with his Southern accent thick. "You need to head outside."

He's the one who loses control. He's the one who hit my mother when she tried to dump out the alcohol. He's the one who swore that this was over. That he wouldn't ever risk hurting us again.

"You shoved me so hard into the wall, my shoulder was so wrecked I couldn't work under the cars for days. You remember that?" I ask him although I don't know why.

I don't know who he is anymore.

I look back up at Miss Jean, who's got her phone in her hand and tears in her eyes. I can't help that my own eyes prick when I say, "A weekly pickup?"

She doesn't look back at my father, who looks to her. All she does is silently nod.

"For how long?" I ask and my father tells me to be quiet. To get out of the store.

After I spent all my time trying to make sure they were okay. I worked extra to make sure they could stay healthy. I didn't tell a soul my father wasn't working anymore. It wasn't a father-son shop anymore.

"How long, Miss Jean?" I repeat and her answer makes me see red.

"As long as I've worked here." She's worked here since before I was born.

Chapter 15

Brianna

BOTH RENEE'S MESSAGE AND THE MUG OF steaming hot chai latte make it seem like it's going to be fine. Like everything in the whole wide world is going to be just fine.

If you want him and he wants you, then just go for it.

I tap out my message and ignore Melissa even though her quick pace to the window gets my attention as I sit in my favorite wicker chair in the bakery.

You make it sound so easy, I text her and then peek up at the menu. The bakery's rolls are heavenly and downtown they buy them by the bulk to pair with their chili. If things are the way they used to be, Asher will get a Reuben and I'm craving a ham and cheddar with spicy mustard. Although I think I might ask Asher if he wants to go out for chili dogs tonight, now that I think about it.

I check my messages from him again to see he hasn't responded to me asking if he's almost here. The clock reads that he's six minutes late, but knowing him he's probably caught up in a conversation. I debate on ordering for him so I'm not late getting back to the office.

My phone pings and it's not Asher.

'*Cause it is*, Renee messages back at the same time that Melissa startles me with a far too loud "hey" and I turn around in my chair, the simplistic yet chic and almost hippie decor blurring as I do, to see Melissa waving me to come over.

"Me?" I question as she practically bounces in her apron that's longer than her blue polka dot minidress or romper, I'm not sure which it is.

My brow furrows as Melissa looks back at me and nearly hisses, "Brianna Ann, get your butt over here." Her tennis shoes stomp as she gives the command.

What in the world? I'd be lying if I said a familiar and unwanted nervousness wasn't spreading over me. The kind you get when you know something isn't right. Like something bad happened. It's in her posture, her tone. Her pointer finger bounces off the front bay window as I'm halfway to her.

"It's Asher." Her eyes are wide and there's nothing but sympathy lingering in her voice.

A chill runs through me as I rush to the window.

The sight is heartbreaking. Mr. Hart shoves Asher. Hard into the parked car and Asher doesn't miss a beat to shove him back.

"What is going—" Melissa's mid-question but I can't stay. My body moves on its own. I shove the small chair that had the unfortunate position of being between myself and the exit and it crashes to the floor as I fling the door open and run out into the street.

Miss Jean is calling down the street. A few other people have made it out to the sidewalk. Griffin and Brody both exit the bar and jog up, they're yelling to stop. A few other people are calling out to break it up.

Heat dances along my skin as I witness Asher land a right hook on his dad's face.

The sight is one I never thought I'd see in my life and judging how Miss Jean backs up, she'd agree.

It's a brawl between son and father on Main Street in broad daylight. My jaw drops as his father cups his cheek and Asher calls him a liar among other words I can barely make out.

"Bri, get him!" Miss Jean yells and Melissa's behind me shouting the same.

My heart pounds as everyone stares.

"How could you!" Asher screams at the same time that I call out his name.

He doesn't hear me, though. If he does, he's not listening.

All I know at this moment is that this isn't like Asher, and he isn't okay. The words are raw as I yell out, "Asher," and he glances back over his shoulder.

His father pushes forward, both arms out, but Brody and Griffin are there, attempting to get between. Everyone's yelling, getting involved or spectating, but all I can see is Asher.

The hurt in his eyes. The bruise on his own jaw.

"Asher!" I call out to him again and this time I don't stop. I don't stop running until my arms are firmly around him. I don't listen to the men when they tell me to step away. To get back.

My own instincts are to stay back, but I can't. Because that leaves Asher in the middle of this. Whatever it is. I don't know what happened, but I don't care.

"Bri, get out of here," Asher warns and attempts to push me away at the same time that someone's hard body presses against mine. Someone's been shoved. Everyone's still yelling but all I hear is Asher, his heavy chaotic breathing and him telling me to let go. He tries again to push me from between him and his father, but I grip my wrists, making a lock of them and refusing to step away.

Closing my eyes, I resign my fate to be where I'm clinging to him.

Asher's grip is tight on me, but I'm tighter in my hold. His voice lowers. "Bri baby, please," he says more calmly, moving back and I feel us hit the car. I don't know whose car and I don't care. I don't care about anything but holding onto him.

One second, it's like we're surrounded; the next, the shade moves and a breeze slips through us.

Griffin's voice tells he's out of breath. "You all right?" He heaves and Brody calls out for someone to go home. I'm assuming Asher's father.

I second-guess everything I saw.

"I'm fine," Asher answers Griffin and I think maybe I can loosen my grip as I open my eyes to see Melissa watching.

The moment she sees me, her worried expression changes into one of authority.

"You all go back to your business," she calls down the street.

Miss Jean does the same. I recognize her voice. "Nothing to see here," she adds.

"You can let go, Bri," Asher whispers, but his tone is different. I don't trust it.

"You need me to do anything? Want me to ..." Griffin offers although it's obvious he doesn't know what he's offering.

"If you could help me get my girlfriend off of me," Asher tries to joke, but his tone is flat again. A short huff of laughter comes from him, but it's just not right.

I loosen my grip and look up at him, ignoring Griffin's attempt to laugh. There's an ache that doesn't quit when I look up at Asher's face. His cheeks are flushed from exertion but that's not why his eyes are red rimmed.

"I'll leave you guys to it," Griffin murmurs.

I reach out slowly and take his hands in mine. He kisses my hair to keep from looking me in the eyes. I know that's why he did it.

When he does, I turn my attention to his injuries. One knuckle is already bruised.

My heart beats slow, and with a pain I can't describe. How can I love this man so damn much, yet have no idea what just happened when it's obvious that it wrecked him?

"Asher," I say and barely get the word out. The hot sun beats down on us and as I look up at Asher, he glances around the sidewalk, as if any of these people matter.

"Asher!" I call his name far louder than I should but it gets his attention. His hazel eyes pierce right into mine. I want to ask him what happened, but those aren't the words that come out. "Are you okay?"

Chapter 16

Asher

MY HANDS ARE STILL SHAKING SLIGHTLY. There's a bruise on my right knuckles that takes up the length of my hand. I try to ignore it as we sit down and I hold the cup of sweet tea Melissa gave me.

"I don't know what the hell happened," I tell Brianna, barely able to look her in the eyes. "Like how it escalated as quickly as it did." My wide-eyed, beautiful woman stares back at me with untold depth in her irises. Like she's shocked and saddened, but more than anything worried for me. Her hand is resting palm up on the corner table in the coffee shop and I'm quick to take it. Even if my hand is battered and bruised, I can hold hers.

"Have you guys—" she starts, her voice low enough

that no one in this place could hear. Even though I'm all too aware Melissa is trying, cleaning mugs that don't need to be wiped down just so she can be as close to us as possible.

I cut Bri off and tell her, "No, we got into it once or twice when he was drunk two years ago …" My breath catches in my throat, remembering how my mother was crying. She just wanted him to stop but she was afraid to get between him and the door.

He was drunk as a skunk, fighting with her and wanting to get in the car and get more beer.

"Once or twice?" Bri questions and I take in a steadying inhale.

"We had a couple of rough months," I admit to her and my thumb runs soothing circles over her knuckles. Readjusting in her seat, she faces me fully and then reaches up to my temple.

Her touch stings and it's only then I realize I must have a cut or a bruise there near my eyebrow.

My eyes feel raw, my muscles are still tense and wound up. But I'm better now.

"I want you to tell me everything, Asher," Brianna murmurs, peering up at me like she's afraid I won't.

As I lean back in the seat, it creaks. Every memory hits me, over and over. I used to not be able to sleep because of them.

A little bit Dirty

Not until Bri would text me to tell her I loved her so she could sleep. And once that was over … I couldn't sleep at all until my father had quit.

"What happened, Asher?"

Melissa comes by just as my mouth parts. "Can I get you two anything?" she asks calmly, with kindness I don't feel I deserve right now.

I know I swung first. I know I did. I started it today.

"We're good. Just need some privacy," Bri answers and again readjusts, this time getting closer to me, holding my one hand with both of hers and moving it to her lap.

"You can tell me, Asher," she says and still I hesitate. My mother doesn't want a soul to know. "Whatever it is, it's going to be okay," she promises me and tears prick the back of my eyes because she doesn't get it. It's not going to be okay.

"He's an alcoholic," I tell her as I sniff and give in to the need of someone else just knowing. Anyone else in this whole damn world. As I lean forward, the legs of the chair scrape against the floor. "Two years ago, maybe a little more." I swallow thickly, looking up at Bri and then dropping my gaze.

"When we were together?" she questions and she doesn't hide the struggle to contain her emotions.

"Yeah, we were together," I admit under my breath, staring at the table.

I expect her hand to fall, or to loosen on mine, but it tightens instead.

"Okay, two years ago, last spring?"

Nodding I look up at her to find her attention all on me, head tilted, wanting me to continue. It's something I haven't had in so damn long. Someone to at least listen. Even if they can't help me. I just want someone to know.

So I tell her how Dad's drinking got worse. How Mom was just trying to take the bottle away from him when he hit her. How instead of him realizing how bad it was getting, he just kept drinking. All day and all night. How my mother tried to stop him, how I had to step in.

How it happened once while Bri was outside and it scared the hell out of me.

I wanted to protect Bri and my mother, and my father too.

"I'm so sorry, Asher," Bri whispers over and over as I go through that first week. I've thought about it so many times.

"I wanted to tell you, but you had your midterms and you wanted me to come up after ..." I can barely swallow the lump in my throat so I force myself to take a sip of sweet tea.

"Asher, I would have dropped them in a heartbeat. They are nothing compared—"

"I know you would have, which I couldn't do to you," I admit to her. "I know you would have done anything for me. I just couldn't have done anything for you, except keep you out of it, far fucking from all that."

Bri is silent, but she doesn't loosen her grip so I add my hand on top of hers. I remember once we sat like this. Back when I first kissed her. In the garage, cross-legged on the concrete floor. My heart raced, I was so afraid to do it wrong. But our hands were just like this and that kiss made her fall in love with me.

I tighten my grip on her now and tell her, "I'm so sorry I couldn't be the man you wanted or the man you needed back then."

"Don't you dare," Bri says, taking her hands away and my whole heart drops until her hands cup around my face and she pulls me in, her nose brushing against mine, her forehead resting against mine. "You don't apologize to me, Asher. Just let me be the woman you need—"

"I don't want you to—" I'm quick to grip her wrists, to keep her from feeling like she's responsible for any of this. Like she has to involve herself.

Pressing her finger to my lips, she stops me and whispers, "It's okay to lean on me."

A moment passes. A beat and then another. Nothing else exists. It's like falling.

Closing my eyes, I rest my forehead against hers and that's just what I do. I let myself fall. My breathing is strangled as I ask her one favor. One thing I need.

"Can you promise me something, though?"

"What?"

I open my eyes and wait for her to do the same, and I practically beg her, "Can you not hate him? Or blame him? He's sick." I barely get the last word out.

The cords in her neck pull as she swallows thickly and nods.

"I know. I know. It's going to be okay."

"I said some things I shouldn't have," I tell her, feeling so damn exhausted out of nowhere.

"We all do, it's going to be okay."

"I told him I hated him."

"Do you?"

"I don't. I hate that he lies. I hate that he drinks. I hate what he does when he's an angry drunk. But I don't hate him. I love him."

"He knows that, Asher. I promise you, he knows that. And you can tell him that too."

It's quiet a moment as we sit back in our seats, our hands still clasped.

I admit the one truth, the one thing I really need

right now. "Fuck, I'm so tired, Bri, and all I know is that I would sleep better if I knew you were going to be there when I woke up in the morning."

"I will. I'm right here."

After another moment, Bri hesitantly asks, "You said you were paying all the bills?"

I nod once, not knowing where she's going with this.

"Did you know he was selling the house?"

"What?" A weight like a ton of bricks hits my chest. "There's no way."

This time she's the one to nod silently.

Time ticks slowly. *Our house? What about the land? The garage is on that land.* Denial and question after question pile up in my head, making it difficult to think straight.

"I was afraid if I left, something would happen … something like him doing something stupid." I speak without thinking, just so she can hear too.

My voice drifts "… But hell, I was right there and I didn't know."

"This isn't your fault," Bri says and there's strength in her admission.

Reaching for my cell in my pocket, I tell Bri, "I have to call my mom." I need to know if she knows what the hell is going on with the house. As far as I knew, the mortgage was being paid. That house has belonged to my mother's family for as long as we've lived in this town. Generations back. Several years back, my parents needed money for unexpected bills, on top of other debts. At least that's what they told me when I saw how much debt they were in. Mom never was good with money, but she at least paid her bills. I thought my father did too. How the hell wasn't the mortgage being paid?

"Okay, I'm here. I'm right here."

As I stand, I bring her hand to my lips and kiss her knuckles and my Bri baby, she stands quickly and wraps her arms around me, tight as all hell before kissing me straight on the lips.

It takes me a second to even realize she's hugging me and not trying to drag me back down, her grip is so tight. A small chuckle leaves me as I wrap my arms around her and run my hands up and down her back in soothing strokes.

My Bri.

I almost tell her I love her, but she beats me to it.

"I love you."

I whisper in her hair before leaving another kiss on her temple. "I know you do. I love you too."

❁

Brianna

The heaviness in my chest doesn't budge. I don't know when it will. As I watch him, pacing outside as he chats on the phone, one hand in his pocket, the one with his bruised knuckles, all I can do is come up with a plan.

I'm at a complete loss, though. Feeling all of four inches tall, all I want to do is text my mom. She has a lawyer who can help Asher with the financials and the deed … his mother, too, although I don't know where she stands on any of this.

I have a cousin who went to rehab and my dad will know the name of that place.

I fiddle with the cup in front of me, feeling nothing but heartache and helpless. And useless. Asher would fix the world for me and all I want to do is fix any of this for him. Any little bit of it, but I will never betray him. Ever.

He's got to be the one to ask my mom. Or to tell me to ask her.

Or we can figure it out on our own. "We'll figure it out," I tell him and heave in the heaviest breath I've ever felt as I remember his father shoving him against the car.

My phone pings and I jump. Startled and once again feeling so damn small.

It's my mom asking where I am. I'm the worst employee ever.

I text back that I can't come in and within a second she texts back, *Don't worry about coming in. Just take care of Asher.*

The need to ask her for help takes over and as it does, she messages, *If there's anything I can do, just ask.*

I'm so busy staring at the text that I don't hear Melissa come up.

"You okay, Bri?" she asks, her hands shoved in the large front pocket of her apron. "You look like you might burst into tears."

Clearing my throat, I steady myself. "I'll be all right, but thanks for asking." I'm polite and putting on the false air that everything's fine somehow makes it feel like it is, even if it's just for a moment.

She leans forward and peeks out front to where Asher is still on the phone. I follow her gaze, feeling so badly for my wounded knight in shining armor. Sometimes it's not the dragons that defeat us, it's the people around us, who we love so dearly, but they're hurting and we can't do anything to stop it.

"What's going on?" Melissa whispers, and I peek at her in the corner of my eye before turning fully to face her.

What a busybody. "Nunya," I answer comically and then reach for my chai that is far too cold, "nunya business."

She has the decency to huff a laugh and throw her hands up. "Fine, fine. But if you need anything, I'm here."

She starts to walk away but I stop her, asking for a really strong coffee.

"Does that mean Baileys?" she asks with a devilish smirk. Alcohol … uh, no. Not at this moment.

"For the love of all things holy, no. Just a big cup, please," I answer her and then think back on the times we've been out. I don't think Asher's been drinking.

More questions pile up and I wish he'd get back here so I can ask him every single one.

"I'll get you the largest mug I've got," Melissa adds a pat to the table and flashes me a full-on charming smile as she leaves.

It's then that the door chimes and Asher comes back in. The cut on his brow looking slightly worse, but overall, he seems better. Calmer and less on edge.

His butt isn't even fully in his seat before my hand is wrapped around his.

We're in this together.

He squeezes my hand and I squeeze his back, but gently so I don't bother his injury.

"Everything okay?" I ask him and he nods, although he still hasn't looked me in the eye.

His focus stays on the table as he taps his phone down on its side, then rotates and taps the top of it nervously.

"I think, if it's all right with you, I'd like to set up a meeting with your mom and my mom's going to come too." He finally looks up at me. "She had no idea about the house going up on the market or my father continuing to drink."

I'm too busy nodding to form words but after a moment of him staring back at me, I clear my throat and tell him, "Of course. I'll message her or do you want to call her? Or come back with me?" All the words rush out without me thinking, just letting them spill.

He nods and says he'll come back to the office with me. His tone is deflated, his expression defeated.

It's more than obvious he feels betrayed. Again, my wheels spin coming up with a plan, anything that can help. He's the fixer in my life and he always has been, but I'll be damned if I don't do everything I can right now to help him.

"Is she staying—" I start to ask, knowing there are some rentals Mrs. Hart can stay in tonight if she just wants to get away. But he cuts me off to say, "My aunt is picking her up. She got there right before I hung up."

"Good, good," I whisper and then, just as I start to offer him to stay with me, he says, "Robert messaged me that I could stay with him."

My heart sinks slightly, a chill going through me. I stare back at him, wanting to say a million things, but mostly to admit that I don't want to be away from him right now.

"Unless, he said, unless I was staying with you tonight."

I can't help the smile that breaks out on my face, although I'm quick to tame it. Licking my lips, I tell him, "Whatever you want to do or wherever you want to go, I just want to be there with you."

An asymmetric grin pulls at his lips and for the first time since all this broke out, I feel relief. He kisses the back of my hand and then turns it over to kiss my wrist.

"Good," he tells me, like that finalizes it although he doesn't give me any details at all.

With the hum of warmth flowing through me, I try to lighten the mood. "You called me your girlfriend." He scoots closer to me, and rests a hand on the inside of my thigh, leaning back and looking more and more like he's okay. Like he's really all right and we're okay.

Like it might all work out.

"You didn't correct me," he murmurs. There's a longing in his hazel eyes and a mischievousness that's all Asher as he peers down at me.

"Like I could?" I joke and my heart aches.

"It's going to get around town now," he presses.

"Looks like you might be stuck with me then," I joke.

He huffs a laugh, pulling me in closer. "Stuck with you? Bri baby, I am never letting you go."

"Good, you better not ... You better not leave me or push me away or keep anything from me, Asher." I toughen my tone slightly, but I've never felt more vulnerable in my life. There is no greater truth in this world than that this man needs me and I need him. Well maybe one, that we love each other.

"There is no way in hell I am ever letting you get away again. I maybe made some mistakes, but I told you, I'm not making them again."

"You meant it when you said it, right? You still love me?" I can't help but question even though I know it's true. I just need to hear him say it.

"I have always loved you," he tells me and I'm quick to say it back and kiss him on the lips, even though Melissa is standing right there, trying to interrupt us with a cup of coffee.

She can see me making out with him. I don't care in the least.

Let the whole damn town see.

I love Asher Hart and I'm going to kiss this man every day for the rest of my life.

Chapter 17

Asher

One week later

THIS HOUSE ISN'T EVEN CLOSE TO BEING done, but lying in bed with Bri makes it feel like home already. The comforter is pulled up around us with the breeze feeling just right as it blows in through the window that's cracked open. Her soft curves are pressed against my body and her arm is wrapped around my chest as I lie on my back while she lies on her side.

Even if the mattress is on the floor and there aren't enough cardboard boxes to fill this place, it's everything I wanted it to be.

We'll fill it up over time and make it feel like ours even though according to Bri, a home is never done. Little by little, we'll make our life together here.

Right here, just the two of us.

"So your mom is coming tomorrow?" Bri whispers and her warm breath tickles my chest. As she readjusts, the mattress creaks under us.

"Mm-hmm." I hum my confirmation and kiss her forehead. Anxiousness creeps through me at the idea of my mom coming home. She only agreed because my father left for rehab. It's one where you have to stay 24/7.

Growing up, I never questioned if my parents loved each other. I always knew they did and hell, they were my role models. My father admitted when his father passed and then his mother in the same year, that's when things went to hell for him. Him acknowledging he has a problem is progress, so I'll take it.

Rubbing a hand down my face, I try not to think about it. Bri sits up, planting a kiss on my collarbone and telling me it's going to be okay. She's a mind reader, I'll tell you that.

"I know, I know," I tell her and my voice is tired.

Hers is just as tired as she settles back down and says, "If you knew that, your heart wouldn't be racing right now."

Staring up at the ceiling, watching the fan spin, I think of what I can possibly say, but Bri says it all for me. "It's okay to be scared, Ash. Too much is out of our control but we can be here for them and I'm here for you," she says the strongest words with the weakest tone as exhaustion threatens to pull her under.

"I love you," she whispers against my chest before yawning.

Kissing her hair, I whisper that I love her too and I nearly let her drift off, but I'm learning to let her in, even into the spots I don't know are safe. The areas of my life I don't know I can fix.

"What if … what if he can't quit it?" I ask her and my throat is tight.

"He can try again," she answers.

"What if my mom doesn't forgive him?"

She hesitates this time and I know why. Neither of us know if my parents will ever be together again. He nearly sold her family's house out from under her. My mom hasn't been doing the best, if I'm being honest.

"I think … when it comes to others, it's more a matter of being there for them so they can heal and if part of their healing is putting up walls …" she's careful with her words, "then you just have to be there for them during that too."

Swallowing thickly, I nod. There's a part of me that blames myself. Like if I'd been stronger, if I'd paid closer attention, I could have stopped it. I could have kept my parents together.

"It's not your fault," Bri whispers and I clear my

throat before telling her that I'm going to be pissed if I find out she can actually read minds.

"I just know you, Asher. You can't fix everything," she adds and kisses me fully this time. Splaying my fingers through her hair, I deepen the kiss. Needing her right now.

"I want to love you forever," I admit to her.

"Well, that's a damn good thing," she says as she nestles down, and lays her cheek on my chest, "'Cause I'll be loving you forever too."

Brianna

As I nuzzle closer, Asher wraps his arm around me. His body's hard and warm, but molds perfectly to mine. Inhaling his masculine scent, I note that this is home. This is exactly where I'm supposed to be. In his arms. In his bed … although I do wish we had a box spring.

"Thank you for making me happy," Asher whispers and it strikes a chord in my heart.

"Always," I tell him, my voice a little too raw with emotion. Moving my knee up and letting my thigh rest on top of him, I joke, "If talking didn't help, I was prepared to distract you with my womanly ways."

Asher's rough chuckle is everything I need right now. Smiling, I peer up at the man I've always loved. His stubble has grown out more than he usually keeps it, and his expression is weighed down with tiredness, but he's happy.

Lying here with me, he's happy. And there's nothing else I could ever want more.

"I think the saying you're looking for is feminine wiles," he corrects me, pulling me closer to him and I know exactly what he's up to.

"If you say so," I tease back, nipping his lip and feeling the warmth between us turn hotter.

He kisses me once and then twice, breathing in deep and heavy as he adjusts me to lie on my back.

His lips find the crook of my neck and his stubble tickles but his touch is fire along my bare skin. "What are you doing?" I ask as if him lifting the covers up so he can duck under them isn't obvious enough.

"I want some dessert before bed. Bri baby, spread your legs for me."

My body obeys instantly, my knees bent as Asher's shoulders lower between them.

I can't help the moan that slips out the moment his tongue massages my clit. Instantly, my nipples are hard and my body tense. With a hand in his hair, I arch my back and groan his name.

"Mmm," he hums into my pussy. "That's my good girl." His voice is throaty and cloaked with desire as he pushes two fingers into me.

My hips buck but he keeps me down with his other hand. He offers me no mercy, no slow buildup. He handles my body like he can do whatever he'd like to it. Stroking my front wall and sucking my clit at the same time lights every nerve ending on fire. A cold sweat comes first and my toes curl as the pleasure builds.

The sweet luxury stirs in the pit of my stomach until all at once, it crashes through my body. All the way down to my toes and up to my lust-filled head.

I don't even realize I'm breathless until Asher's on top of me, kissing me ravenously and I do everything I can to kiss him back just as passionately.

Gripping my inner thigh, he brings my right leg up and without warning, slams inside of me to the hilt. "Fuck!" I cry out, my bottom lip dropping and the painful sting of pleasure crashing down over the former waves. Heightening it, prolonging it as he rides through my orgasm, pushing for more and taking all that he'd like.

Epilogue

Brianna

"**S**O YOU TWO ARE *TOGETHER*, TOGETHER?" My lips quirk up at the way Renee said the second "together." Broadening my smile, I peer up at her from where I'm perched on my stool at the bar.

"Together together," I answer giddily.

"How did I hear that through a rumor rather than through you?"

"Griffin's as bad as the women at the beauty parlor," I say under my breath, staring across the bar at the back of his head.

I shrug and tell her, "I just didn't want to say it out loud and jinx it, you know?"

"Pretty sure Asher sent out a memo in all caps and

screamed it at Town Hall," Renee jokes and I laugh into my Pepsi.

It's been two solid weeks of every night with Asher, every day getting better and better even though each has its own challenges. We're getting there, though, not back to where we once were, but closer than we ever thought we could be.

Everything else in the town is the same as it's always been, or so it seems. If there's a moment of quiet in conversation it's filled with a gentle, *if you need anything, you let me know*. Asher's always been there with a kind smile and a toolbelt fixing everything for everyone, and to see them gather around him right now, even if he doesn't want to accept any help but mine, means the world to me.

"So now what?" Renee asks and brings me back to the present.

"What do you mean?"

"What's the plan? Salon? Real estate? A marriage and kids and a picket fence?"

My nose scrunches at the thought of a wedding right now. Magnolia just had hers and it was beautiful. I used to think I'd love a wedding one day, and a little one like her Bridget.

With everything Asher's going through and what

his family's going through, I don't see that happening. "I'd be fine if we never got married, to be honest."

"Really?" Renee's genuine shock is surprising.

"I thought you didn't even like weddings?" I question her with a comical tone.

"I mean, I don't. But you and Asher ... you've had your wedding planned since high school, haven't you?"

Just the mention of the two of us in high school brings a soft smile to my face.

"I had a lot of plans half a decade ago, Renee." Remembering back then and how simple everything was, and how little we were prepared. I had lots of ideas and no real idea what they meant. "We all did. Plans change, though. As long as I have Asher, the rest doesn't matter."

"If you say so," Renee says and sighs, like she doesn't believe me.

Her focus drifts and I peek over my shoulder to see Griffin coming through the side door. A stack of papers in one hand, what appears to be an empty coffee cup in the other, and his dark brown eyes on Renee.

His lips lift in the semblance of a smile, like he can't hold it back and I'm quick to turn around and find Renee blushing. She clears her throat and goes back to wiping down bottles.

"Good to see you, Bri," Griffin calls out and gives

me a wave before pushing open the front door. The daylight spills into the dimly lit bar.

"You too, thanks for letting me in early," I tell him and he only nods, his gaze slipping back to Renee before he heads out.

"Yeah, plans never work out like they're supposed to," Renee states, taking in a deep, steadying breath.

"What about you two?"

Her hazel eyes meet mine. "What about who?"

I can't help the smile that breaks out. "You and Griffin?"

She tries to play dumb, but right then and there, she spills it.

And holy hell, love is … something else.

Renee and Griffin's story is up next!
Kiss Me in this Small Town is coming Feb 2024

But first, have you read Magnolia's story?
Tequila Rose is out now!

About the Author

Thank you so much for reading my romances. I'm just a stay at home mom and avid reader turned author and I couldn't be happier.

I hope you love my books as much as I do!

More by Willow Winters
WWW.WILLOWWINTERSWRITES.COM/BOOKS

Made in the USA
Middletown, DE
10 October 2023

40463086R00120